365
Stories and Rhymes for Boys

Illustrated by Andy Everitt-Stewart, Ruth Galloway, Martin Remphry, and Jan Smith.

Additional illustrations by John Bendall Brunello, Bill Bolton, Andy Catling, Caroline Jayne Church, Jacqueline East, Frank Endersby, Daniel Howarth, Steve Smallman, Kristina Stephenson, and Claire Tindall.

Written by Cecil Frances Alexander, Tina Barrett, Janet Allison Brown, Lewis Carroll, Charles F. Carryl, Kate Cary, Deborah Chancellor, Andy Charman, Arthur Hugh Clough, Geoff Cowan, Meryl Doney, Nick Ellsworth, Gaby Goldsack, Kenneth Grahame, Jillian Harker, Ann Harth, Heather Henning, James Hogg, Liz Holliday, Janey Joseph, Claire Keene, Karen King, Rudyard Kipling, Alison Milford, Jan Payne, Beatrice Phillpotts, Ronne Randall, Willam Brighty Rands, Caroline Repchuck, Christina Rossetti, Kath Smith, Louisa Somerville, Robert Louis Stevenson, Christine Tagg, Edward Thomas, Gordon Volke, Candy Wallace, Maureen Warner, and Kat Wootton.

Every effort has been made to acknowledge the contributors to this book. If we have made any errors, we will be pleased to rectify them in future editions.

This edition published by Parragon Books Ltd in 2016 and distributed by

Parragon Inc.
440 Park Avenue South, 13th Floor
New York, NY 10016
www.parragon.com

ISBN 978-1-4748-1213-9

Printed in China

365
Stories
and
Rhymes
for
Boys

PaRragon

Bath · New York · Cologne · Melbourne · Delhi
Hong Kong · Shenzhen · Singapore

Contents

Contents

Contents

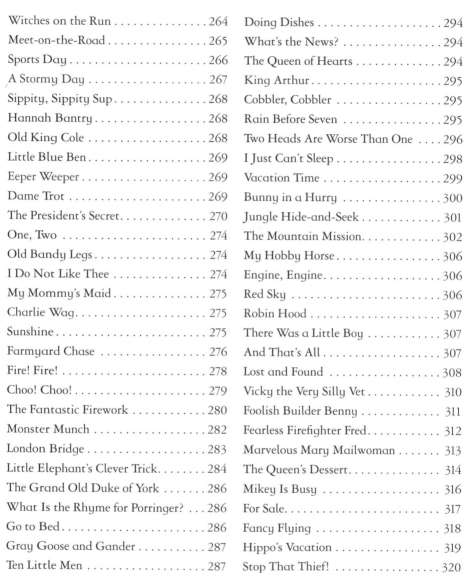

Contents

Shadow's Lucky Charm

Dark shadows of evening hung over the television studios. Bustling by day, now the place stood empty. Only Sam, the security officer, remained. His flashlight shone as he made his rounds, checking everything was shut down.

As he stepped into Studio One, Sam shivered. Why was it always so cold in there? Sam didn't wait to find out. He felt he was being watched.

No sooner had he gone, than...

"Lights, cameras, action!" called Click, a ghostly producer. A creepy cast began to play their parts in the spooky soap opera, *Haunted House*, followed feverishly by ghosts everywhere.

"I can't pretend to be a scary phantom," hissed Gray Ghost to Camera Two.

"I haven't got the spirit for it!"

"Well, don't tell anybody!" smiled Shadow, delivering her lines in the lead role. "It'll be our secret. Besides..."

Suddenly, she froze.

"What's wrong?" asked Gray Ghost.

"I'm going to have to leave the show," said Shadow, unhappily. "I've lost my lucky wishbone. I can't go on without it—I get terrible stage fright."

So *Haunted House* didn't transmit that night.

Early next evening, the sweetest phantom cat Shadow had ever seen stepped through the wall of the studio.

"Who are you?" asked Shadow, curiously.

"I'm Lucky," purred the cat. "I move as silently as a shadow."

"Shadow is my name!" laughed Shadow.

"I've always wanted to be in a TV show," meowed Lucky.

"I want to be out of one," replied Shadow, sadly explaining.

Lucky looked thoughtful. "I've just had a *purrr-fect* idea," he said, whispering into Shadow's ear.

Shadow let out a spine-chilling shriek of joy.

"Shadow, are you all right?" asked Gray Ghost.

"I am now," smiled Shadow.

"Lights, cameras, action!" called Click, when filming on *Haunted House* began the next night.

This time, there was an extra ghost in the high-spirited cast. Lucky was delighted with his glide-on part, and Shadow was even happier about it—her faultless performance proved it. After all, she had a new Lucky charm.

And as for any stage fright, there simply wasn't a ghost of a chance it would return now!

Witch's Brew

Eye of lizard, toe of frog,
Tail of rat, and bark of dog.
Sneeze of chicken, cough of bat,
Lick of weasel, smell of cat.
Stir it up and mix it well,
To make a magic monster spell.

Now it's done, the spell is ready,
The monster's rising, slow and steady.
"Pleased to meet you," Winnie sighs.
"Pleased to eat you," he replies.
What's gone wrong, she cannot tell,
To spoil the magic monster spell.

The witch goes pale, she must act fast,
Or else this day may be her last!
She grabs her wand. She has a notion
Of how to get rid of this potion.
She shakes her wand, which breaks the spell,
And waves the monster fond farewell!

A Spelling Lesson

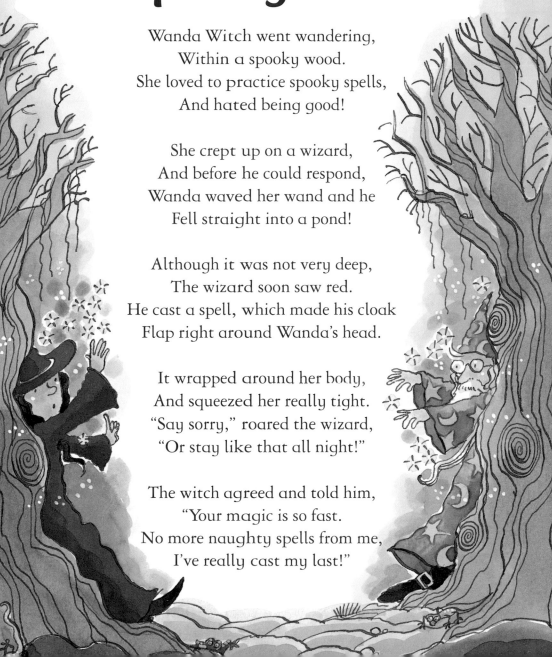

Wanda Witch went wandering,
Within a spooky wood.
She loved to practice spooky spells,
And hated being good!

She crept up on a wizard,
And before he could respond,
Wanda waved her wand and he
Fell straight into a pond!

Although it was not very deep,
The wizard soon saw red.
He cast a spell, which made his cloak
Flap right around Wanda's head.

It wrapped around her body,
And squeezed her really tight.
"Say sorry," roared the wizard,
"Or stay like that all night!"

The witch agreed and told him,
"Your magic is so fast.
No more naughty spells from me,
I've really cast my last!"

Fee, Fi, Fo, Fum!

Fee, fi, fo, fum,
I smell the blood
Of an Englishman
Be he alive or be he dead,
I'll grind his bones
To make my bread.

Little Hare

Round about there
Sat a little hare,
The bow-wows came and chased him
Right up there!

Ten O'Clock Scholar

A diller, a dollar,
A ten o'clock scholar,
What makes you come so soon?
You used to come at ten o'clock,
But now you come at noon.

Round About

Round about the rose bush,
Three steps,
Four steps,
All the little boys and girls
Are sitting
On the doorsteps.

The Magpie

Magpie, magpie, flutter and flee,
Turn up your tail and good luck come to me.

John Smith

Is John Smith within?
Yes, that he is.
Can he set a shoe?
Aye, marry, two;
Here a nail and there a nail,
Tick, tack, too.

I Wish...

I wish I were an elephant,
When it's time for a scrub.
I'd use my nose like a garden hose
To rinse myself in the tub.

I wish I were a chameleon,
Chameleons are best.
I'd change my color and life would be fuller,
For a change is as good as a rest.

I wish I were a dolphin,
A dolphin would be my wish.
Leaping and splashing, I'd be very dashing,
And bathe with all the fish.

I wish I were an ostrich,
An ostrich would be grand.
But if I got scared, would I be prepared
To bury my head in the sand?

I wish I had more wishes,
But now my game is through,
I'm happy to be quite simply me,
Enjoying a day at the zoo.

The Nutty Professor

Professor Von Bean was very excited. He had finished
building his machine and it was ready to use. It was the most
complicated contraption he had ever built.

The professor called his assistant to come to watch him start
the machine. The wheels were green and brown, and there
were levers on either side. The side panels were striped red and
white, and there was a big chimney on the top for the smoke to
escape. There was a cupboard on the side which, the professor
explained, was to hang a wet coat in. There was a shelf on the
back for a box of plants.

While Professor Von Bean was getting more and
more excited, his assistant looked very worried.

"But what does it do?" he asked, timidly.

The professor scratched his head and thought.

"Oh dear, oh dear!" he sighed. "What a fool
I have been! Why didn't I think of that? It
does absolutely nothing useful at all!"

The Cow

The friendly cow all red and white,
I love with all my heart:
She gives me cream with all her might,
To eat with apple tart.

She wanders lowing here and there,
And yet she cannot stray,
All in the pleasant open air,
The pleasant light of day.

And blown by all the winds that pass
And wet with all the showers,
She walks among the meadow grass
And eats the meadow flowers.

The Field Mouse

Where the acorn tumbles down,
Where the ash tree sheds its berry,
With your fur so soft and brown,
With your eye so round and merry,
Scarcely moving the long grass,
Field mouse, I can see you pass.

Field mouse, field mouse, do not go,
Where the farmer stacks his treasure,
Find the nut that falls below,
Eat the acorn at your pleasure,
But you must not steal the grain
He has stacked with so much pain.

Make your hole where mosses spring,
Underneath the tall oak's shadow,
Pretty, quiet, harmless thing,
Play about the sunny meadow.
Keep away from corn and house,
None will harm you, little mouse.

Tractor Trouble

Farmer Fred sped off on the tractor to his first job of the day.
"Woof! Woof!" barked Patch as the tractor whizzed past at
high speed. The tractor was going too fast!
In the next field, Harry Horse trotted
over to see what the noise was about.
He stuck his head over the fence just
as the tractor rushed past.

"Yuck!" neighed Harry, as he
was splattered with lumps of
sticky mud.

But Farmer Fred didn't hear.
He was already on his way to his
next job—collecting bales of hay to feed the cows with.

In no time at all, Farmer Fred had hitched up the trailer of
hay to the tractor.

"We'll have those cows fed before you can say dandelions,"
smiled Farmer Fred.

Farmer Fred rushed across Cowslip Meadow. The hay bales
bounced this way and that. Patch raced after them.

"Woof! Woof!" barked Patch. The hay bales didn't look
safe. But it was too late. A hay bale bounced off the trailer
toward Connie Cow.

"Moo!" cried poor Connie as she jumped into the brook to
avoid a tumbling bale of hay.

"We've finished all our jobs in record time!" said Farmer

Fred as he arrived in the barnyard. "Now, where is everyone?"

Farmer Fred looked around the yard, but he couldn't see any of the animals.

Just then, Patch came running into the yard. "Woof! Woof!" he barked.

"What is it, Patch?" asked Farmer Fred, puzzled. "Do you know where everyone has gone?"

Farmer Fred followed Patch out of the yard. Harry Horse, Polly Pig, Shirley Sheep, and Hetty Hen were standing beside the brook.

Farmer Fred couldn't believe his eyes when he saw Connie Cow stuck in the brook.

"Blithering beets!" Farmer Fred gasped. "How did you get in there?"

"Moo!" said Connie Cow crossly.

"Never fear," said Farmer Fred, cheerfully, as he disappeared into the barn. "I have an idea!"

"I hope poor Connie is rescued soon," said Polly Pig. "You know how her milk curdles when she's upset!"

Just then, the door to the barn flew open and out came Farmer Fred, dragging...

"...The Inflatable Cow-floater," said Farmer Fred proudly. And off he bumped towards the brook.

Harry Horse and the others followed at a safe distance.

Within minutes, Farmer Fred had launched his Inflatable Cow-floater and was busy telling Connie Cow to climb aboard.

The animals held their breath as Connie Cow wibbled and wobbled on top of the Inflatable Cow-floater.

Then there was a scraping sound and a loud hiss.

Connie Cow and the Inflatable Cow-floater sank back into the water.

"Patch," clucked Hetty Hen. "We have to rescue poor Connie."

"I'd pull her out myself, but," sighed Harry Horse, "I'm not as young as I was."

"The tractor is the only one who can help her now," Polly Pig grunted.

"Woof, woof!" barked Patch, picking up the rope attached to the back of the tractor.

"That's it! I have an even better idea!" shouted Farmer Fred. "I know just how to rescue Connie."

Farmer Fred drove the

tractor down to the edge of the brook. He tied the rope to the Cow-floater.

"Poor Connie," mumbled Harry Horse, shaking his mud-splattered head.

Slowly and carefully, Farmer Fred pulled the Cow-floater out of the brook. At last, Connie Cow was safe on dry land. All the animals cheered.

Later, in the barnyard, Farmer Fred was feeling very pleased with himself.

"Look!" he said, showing Jenny the list all checked off, "I've finished all the jobs… and thanks to the tractor, I've had time to rescue Connie!"

Jenny looked at Patch and smiled.

Tom, He Was a Piper's Son

Tom, he was a piper's son,
He learned to play when he was young,
And the only tune that he could play,
Was, "Over the hills and far away."
Over the hills and a great way off,
The wind shall blow my topknot off!

The Squirrel

The winds they did blow,
The leaves they did wag;
Along came a beggar boy,
And put me in his bag.

He took me to London,
A lady me did buy,
Put me in a silver cage,
And hung me up on high.

With apples by the fire,
And nuts for me to crack,
Besides a little feather bed
To rest my little back.

Go to Bed, Tom

Go to bed, Tom, go to bed, Tom,
Tired or not, Tom, go to bed, Tom.

Round and Round the Garden

Round and round the garden,
Like a teddy bear.
One step, two steps,
Tickly under there!

Charley Warley

Charley Warley had a cow,
Black and white about the brow;
Open the gate and let her through,
Charley Warley's old cow.

Daddy

Bring Daddy home with a fiddle and a drum,
A pocket full of spices, an apple, and a plum.

Monster Marathon

"Very nice," said Cyril the Cyclops, eyeing his reflection in a puddle. He was wearing running shoes, running shorts, and a running top. Cyril the Cyclops had entered the annual Monster Marathon, and he had his eye on the trophy.

On the other side of Monster Mountain, two mischievous goblins were busy planning their own strategy for the big race. Booger and Burp were identical twin brothers, and only their mother could tell them apart.

"So," Booger was saying, "we'll swap at the crooked tree."

"That's the plan," agreed Burp.

The day of the Monster Marathon dawned. A large banner saying *ANNUAL MONSTER MARATHON* fluttered in the breeze, and the field was steadily filling up with all kinds of monsters. Cyril watched as a troop of trolls jogged by wearing matching sweatsuits with Team Troll neatly embroidered on the back, looking very professional. He suddenly felt nervous.

The stout monster official raised the starting gun into the still air. There was a deafening hush followed by a gunshot, and the monsters were off!

Cyril did his best, but as he approached the halfway mark he could go no further. It was no good, he had to rest. He slumped down by the side of a crooked tree and almost immediately nodded off—but only moments later he was disturbed by voices.

"It's OK, he's sound asleep," someone said. Cyril kept very still and opened his eye just enough to see the goblin twins swapping clothes and Booger sprinting off into the distance.

Cyril knew what was going on. He had to get to the monster official and tell him what he had seen before it was too late. As soon as Burp had gone, too, he jumped up and ran

as fast as his tired legs could carry him. He reached the finish line just in time to see the trophy being presented to a grinning Booger.

"*Stop!*" shrieked Cyril. "They're cheats!"

In a breathless voice Cyril explained what had happened.

"Nonsense," complained Burp, "I'm his coach. My brother won fair and square."

The monster official gazed from one goblin to the other.

"Then why," he said slowly, pointing to Burp's T-shirt, "are your clothes on inside out?"

And although Cyril hadn't won the race, he was awarded an extra-special trophy for his vigilance and sense of fair play.

Tractor's Busy Day

Here's the tractor, shiny and new.
Chug chug chug! There's so much to do.

The tractor starts a busy day,
Delivering sacks of bales and hay.

Bumpety-bump! The ground is rough,
But the tractor's wheels are wide and tough.

Slow and careful, big and strong,
The tractor tows the trailer along.

The tractor crosses up and down,
Plowing the field, all muddy and brown.

Well done, Tractor! *Chug chug chug!*
Now home to the barn where it's warm and snug.

Tugboat

The tugboat blows his horn to say,
Toot! Toot! Toot! Please make way!

Little Tugboat's tough and strong,
He's built to tow big ships along.

Pushing, pulling! Tug! Tug! Tug!
Backward, forward! *Chug! Chug! Chug!*

Tugboat guides a ship to shore,
Then off he goes to help some more.

Tugboat never gets out of puff,
Even when the waves are rough!

Rain or sunshine, wind or fog—
Toot! Toot! Tugboat loves his job!

Bone Crazy

Alfie sat in his basket chewing on a large bone. Mmm! It tasted good.

When he had chewed it for long enough, he took it down to the bottom of the yard to bury it in his favorite spot beneath the old oak tree. He didn't see next-door's dog, Ferdy, watching him through a hole in the fence.

The next day, when Alfie went to dig up his bone, it was gone! He dug all around, but it was nowhere to be found. Then, he spied a trail of muddy paw prints leading to the fence, and he guessed what had happened.

Alfie was too big to fit through the fence and get his bone back, so he thought of a plan instead. The next day he buried another bone. This time, he knew Ferdy was watching him.

Later, Alfie hid and watched as Ferdy crept into the yard and started to dig up the bone. Suddenly, Ferdy yelped in pain. The bone had bitten his nose! He flew across the yard and through the fence, leaving the bone behind.

Alfie's friend Mole crept out from where the bone was buried. How the two friends laughed at their trick! And from then on, Ferdy always kept safely to his side of the fence.

One Stormy Night

It was Patch's first night outside in his fancy new doghouse. He snuggled down on his blanket and watched as dusk fell.

Before long he fell sound asleep. As he slept, big spots of rain began to fall. A splash of water dripped from the doghouse roof onto his nose.

Then there was a great crash and a bright flash of light lit up the sky.

Patch woke up with a start and was on his feet at once, growling and snarling. "Just a silly storm," he told himself. "Nothing to scare a farm dog!"

But as the lightning flashed yet again, he saw a great shadow looming against the barn. Patch gulped. Whatever could it be? He began to bark furiously, trying to act braver than he felt—and sure enough, next time the lightning flashed, there was no sign of the shadow. "I sure scared that monster away!" he thought.

But as Patch settled back down, the sky outside lit up once more. There in the doorway towered the monster!

"Just checking you're okay in the storm," said Mommy.

"A fearless farm dog like me?" said Patch. "Of course I am!" But as the storm raged on, he snuggled up close to her all the same!

The Lost Rocket

Ethan stared out of the window at Mom's brand-new space rocket.

It had blue and silver stripes and shone in the starlight.

Ethan really wanted to fly it. But he knew Mom wouldn't let him.

Mom put on her space helmet. "I'm off to the space station now, Ethan," she said. "Be good." She stepped into the teleporter, and disappeared into thin air.

Ethan looked at the space rocket. "I could fly that rocket now," he said to himself. "I bet it's really easy." He put on his space suit, went out to the rocket, and slid open the door.

Mom had left the starter crystal in the ignition pad.

Once the door was safely closed, Ethan took off his helmet and pushed down the crystal. The rocket's

engines fired up. Ethan gulped. It was now or never.

"I'll be back by lunch time," he thought.

At first everything seemed easy. Ethan made it safely past planet Earth, and began to head for Mars. But then a comet came rushing toward Ethan. He grabbed the controls, but he couldn't make the rocket swerve away quickly enough. He was going to crash!

"What on Earth are you doing, you naughty boy?"

It was Mom! She was right next to Ethan.

She grabbed the controls and the rocket swerved away from the comet, just in time. "I picked up your SOS, and teleported myself here extra-quick," Mom said.

Mom looked at Ethan. "Just wait until I get you home!" she said with an angry frown. Ethan had a feeling he might be grounded for a very long time. But for once, he didn't mind too much!

If You Hold My Hand

Oakey's mom opened the front door. "Come on, Oakey. Let's go outside and explore."

But Oakey wasn't really sure. He was only small, and the world looked big and scary.

"Only if you promise to hold my hand," said Oakey.

"This looks like a great place to play. Should we take a look? What do you say?" asked Oakey's mom.

"Only if you promise to hold my hand," said Oakey. And Oakey did it!

"This slide looks like fun. Would you like to try?" asked Oakey's mom.

"I'm only small," said Oakey. "I don't know if I can climb that high—unless you hold my hand."

And Oakey did it! "*Wheee!* Did you see me?" he cried.

"We'll take a short cut through the woods," said Oakey's mom.

"I'm not sure if we should," said Oakey. "It looks dark in there. Well, I suppose we could—will you hold my hand?"

And Oakey did it! "*Boo!* I scared you!" he cried.

Deep in the woods, Oakey found a stream, shaded by beautiful tall trees.

"Stepping stones, look!" said Oakey's mom. "Do you think you could jump across these?"

"Maybe," said Oakey. "I just need you to hold my hand, please."

And Oakey did it!

Beyond the woods, Oakey and his mom ran up the hill, and all the way down to the ocean.

"Come on, Oakey," called his mom. "Would you like to wade in the ocean with me?" But the ocean looked big, and he was only small.

Suddenly, Oakey knew that didn't matter at all.

He turned to his mom and smiled… "I can do anything if you hold my hand," he said.

Two Little Dicky Birds

Two little dicky birds sitting on a wall,
One named Peter, one named Paul.
Fly away, Peter!
Fly away, Paul!
Come back, Peter!
Come back, Paul!

Once I Saw a Little Bird

Once I saw a little bird
Come hop, hop, hop,
So I cried, "Little bird,
Will you stop, stop, stop?"
And was going to the window,
To say, "How do you do?"
But he shook his little tail,
And far away he flew.

Little Robin Redbreast

Little Robin Redbreast
Sat upon a rail:
Niddle-noddle went his head!
Wiggle-waggle went his tail.

Intery, Mintery, Cutery, Corn

Intery, mintery, cutery, corn,
Apple seed and apple thorn.
Wire, briar, limber, lock,
Three geese in a flock.

One flew east and one flew west;
One flew over the cuckoo's nest.

The North Wind Doth Blow

The north wind doth blow,
And we shall have snow,
And what will poor Robin do then?
Poor thing!

He'll sit in a barn,
And to keep himself warm,
Will hide his head under his wing.
Poor thing!

Magpies

One for sorrow, two for joy,
Three for a girl, four for a boy,
Five for silver, six for gold,
Seven for a secret never to be told.

Clumsy Fred

Clumsy Fred seemed to be a very cross and very clumsy giant!
He bumped into castles and turned homes into rubble. He
sent cars flying as he strode across the town, and he
stepped on lampposts, demolishing them.

The townspeople were very concerned. What
was the matter with Fred? He didn't use to be so
cross and clumsy. There was definitely something
wrong, but no one was sure how to help.

Then a monster expert came to the rescue. He
went to see Fred in his cave above the town.

Fred was feeling very sorry for himself. "Why
am I so clumsy?" he asked. "I don't like upsetting
everyone, but I just can't help it!"

The expert did a lot of tests. Finally he
found the solution. "I know what is wrong!"
he said. "The problem is your eye. You're
near-sighted!"

The expert gave Fred a monocle to try
out. "I can see!" he cried.

And that was the end of Clumsy Fred!

Not Another Bear

Tyler loved teddy bears. When asked what he would like for his birthday, or Christmas, Tyler's answer was always the same: "A teddy bear, please!"

"Not another bear!" his parents would say. "Look at your bed, Tyler. There's no room for any more!"
It was true. There were bears all over Tyler's bed. Every night Tyler had to squeeze into the tiny space that was left. But Tyler didn't mind at all.

"We've got to do something about this," said Tyler's dad, one day, marching into Tyler's bedroom with a pile of wood and a bag of tools. By dinner time there were three shelves on Tyler's bedroom wall, and a row of bears sat neatly on each one.

Next day was the school fair. As they walked in, Mom gave Tyler some pocket money. "Find something you'd like to buy," she said.

"What did you buy, Tyler?" Mom asked, when they got home. Tyler grinned.

"Not another bear!" sighed Mom.

"But there's plenty of room now," Tyler answered. He winked at the new bear. And Tyler was sure that the bear winked back!

Princess Prissy

King Fusspot liked everything to be just so. He had his own Rule Book, covering such vital matters as the number of brush strokes his daughter Princess Prissy's royal hair should receive before bed.

Secretly, Princess Prissy thought that her father's Rule Book was just silly, but she never dared to say anything.

Now the Stinky Bog Monster had never read the Rule Book. So when he crashed through Princess Prissy's window one dark night, he didn't give a second thought to the broken glass, crumpled covers, and slimy trail he was leaving behind him, as he carried the princess off kicking and screaming.

"My poor daughter!" wailed King Fusspot the next morning. "Stuck in that stinking, disorganized lair!"

This was too good a chance to miss for Prince Smarmy. He swiftly struck a deal with the king, ensuring the princess's hand in marriage in return for her safe rescue.

Now, Prince Smarmy knew King Fusspot's Rule Book well, and knew all the proper procedures to follow when rescuing princesses. One very important rule was that a prince had to appear on a gleaming white charger. It was when he was hiding behind a tree outside the Bog Monster's lair, cleaning the mud off his horse, that the prince caught sight of Princess Prissy.

Her clothes were torn and covered in stains, and her hair was a filthy mess. The prince's heart was torn with anguish. His darling princess—what had that nasty Bog Monster done to her?

Just then, as he prepared to leap onto his charger to rescue her, the Bog Monster himself appeared.

"Hello there, Boggy darling!" cried Princess Prissy. And with that, she planted a kiss on his cheek! The prince cried out in horror.

"Not you!" cried the princess, catching sight of Prince Smarmy. "If you've come to rescue me, get lost! I'm not coming home—ever! At last I've escaped all those silly rules. All that niceness, and prettiness, and good manners. I'm free! I like being rude and horrible. I've got my darling Stinky Bog Monster to thank for it, and you're too late—we got married last night!"

There was nothing else to do. Prince Smarmy had to admit defeat and head home.

On the way, he noticed a muddy puddle in front of him.

"Why not?" he thought, and rode his horse straight through it, splattering both of them with mud. He laughed out loud. "You never know," he thought. "Perhaps the princess was right, after all. Some rules are just silly."

And he rode through every single puddle all the way home.

Chalk and Cheese

Chalk and Cheese were as different as two kittens can be. Chalk was fluffy and white. She liked dishes of cream and lazing in the sun. Cheese was a rough, tough black kitten. He liked chewing on fish bones and climbing trees. Their mother puzzled over her odd little kittens, but she loved them both the same.

One day, Cheese climbed high up on the barn and got stuck. "Help!" he cried to his sister.

"I don't like climbing!" she said, opening one eye.

"If only you were like me," said Cheese, "you could help!"

"If only you were like me," said Chalk, "you wouldn't have gotten stuck!" And with that she went back to sleep.

Just then, the farm dog came by. Chalk sprang up as he gave a loud bark and began to chase her.

"Help!" she cried to Cheese, up on the barn.

"I'm stuck, remember?" he cried. "You shouldn't lie where dogs can chase you."

Then Mommy appeared. She swiped the dog away with her claws, then climbed up and rescued Cheese.

"If only you were both more like me," she said, "you'd keep out of danger and look after each other."

And from then on, that's just what they did.

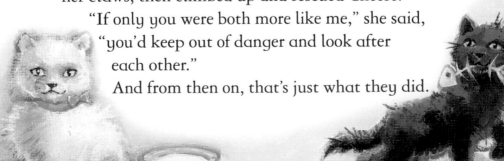

Oscar the Octopus

Oscar the Octopus was a keen soccer player. With his many feet he was a real menace to the other team.

Oscar began to get ready for today's big game. He stretched out a tentacle and put on the first shoe, then he put on the second. As Oscar put on shoe three, the crowds had begun to gather beside the ocean to watch the game. He could hear them singing soccer songs.

On went shoe five as the crowd swayed and cheered loudly. The harder Oscar tried to hurry, the longer it seemed to take!

Shoe number six went on, and Oscar stood on his head and practiced some tricks, then shoe seven—he was almost ready. Now it was the last one—shoe eight. Oscar was getting nervous and the laces were so tricky that it took him ages.

At last he was ready and onto the field he went.

But the referee said, "Sorry, Oscar! You're too late. The game is over, the whistle has blown. Nobody scored and the crowd has gone home!"

The Camel's Complaint

Canary birds feed on sugar and seed,
Parrots have crackers to crunch;
And, as for the poodles, they tell me the noodles
Have chickens and cream for their lunch.
But there's never a question
About *my* digestion—
Anything does for me!

Cats, you're aware, can repose in a chair,
Chickens can roost upon rails;
Puppies are able to sleep in a stable,
And oysters can slumber in pails.
But no one supposes a poor camel dozes—
Any place does for me!

Lambs are enclosed where it's never exposed,
Coops are constructed for hens;
Kittens are treated to houses well-heated,
And pigs are protected by pens.
But a camel comes handy
Wherever it's sandy—
Anywhere does for me!

People would laugh if you rode a giraffe,
Or mounted the back of an ox;
It's nobody's habit to ride on a rabbit,
Or try to bestraddle a fox.
But as for a camel, he's ridden by families—
Any load does for me!

A snake is as round as a hole in the ground,
And weasels are wavy and sleek;
And no alligator could ever be straighter
Than lizards that live in a creek.
But a camel's all lumpy
And bumpy and humpy—
Any shape does for me!

Tina the House Robot

It was Saturday morning. Ethan's little sister was late for her moon-dancing class.

"Hurry up, Zelda!" said Mom. "It's time to go!" She went to get Zelda's space suit and found Ethan's lying on the floor.

"Your space suit is dirty, Ethan. Can you wash it please?" Mom shouted, as she rushed out of the house with Zelda.

Ethan looked at his space suit. He really didn't feel like washing it. Then he had an idea.

Ethan gave Tina the House Robot his space suit, and pressed "wash" on her control panel.

Immediately Tina started washing the suit. It was all so easy. Ethan went to watch Star Search on the couch. He soon fell asleep.

Ethan woke feeling uncomfortable. He was sitting in a puddle of water. Tina had washed his space suit, but she hadn't stopped there. She had washed the whole house from top to bottom, and everything was covered in soap bubbles.

What a terrible mess!

Ethan looked at his watch. Mom would be back soon. In a panic, he selected Tina's "power dry" setting, and switched her speed up to "very fast."

Tina whizzed around as fast as her wheels would spin, drying everything in sight with blasts of hot air.

The front door opened. Mom and Zelda were home. Ethan pushed Tina into the kitchen and ran to meet them.

Mom was holding something shiny in her hand. "What have you done to your space suit?" she asked. Tina's hot air had shrunk his space suit to half its size.

"I should tell you off," said Mom, "but I won't, because you have cleaned the house so well!"

Ethan started to tell her that Tina had done it all, then changed his mind. "No problem," he smiled.

Ducks' Ditty

All along the backwater,
Through the rushes tall,
Ducks are a-dabbling,
Up tails all!

Ducks' tails, drakes' tails,
Yellow feet a-quiver,
Yellow bills all out of sight
Busy in the river!

Slushy green undergrowth
Where the roach swim
Here we keep our larder,
Cool and full and dim.

Every one for what he likes!
We like to be
Heads down, tails up,
Dabbling free!

High in the blue above
Swifts whirl and call.
We are down a-dabbling,
Up tails all!

The Kangaroo

Old Jumpety-Bumpety-Hop-and-Go-One
Was lying asleep on his side in the sun.
This old kangaroo, he was whisking the flies
(With his long glossy tail) from his ears and his eyes.
Jumpety-Bumpety-Hop-and-Go-One
Was lying asleep on his side in the sun,
Jumpety-Bumpety-Hop!

The Three Billy Goats Gruff

Once upon a time there were three Billy Goats Gruff. There was a big goat, a middle-sized goat, and a little goat.

The three goats all loved to eat grass. They ate grass all day long on the hill. But they never crossed the bridge to eat the grass on the other side, because a troll lived under the bridge.

One day the little Billy Goat Gruff looked at the green grass on the other side of the bridge. "I'm not scared of a silly old troll," he said. "I'm going to cross the bridge."

So the little Billy Goat Gruff set off across the bridge.

Trip, trap, trip, trap went his hooves.

"Who's that trip-trapping over my bridge?" roared the troll.

"It's only me!" said the little Billy Goat Gruff. "I'm going to eat the green grass on the other side of the bridge."

"Oh no, you're not!" roared the troll. "I'm going to eat you up!"

"But I'm just little," said the little Billy Goat Gruff. "Wait until the middle-sized goat comes across."

So the little Billy Goat Gruff crossed the bridge.

Next, the middle-sized Billy Goat Gruff crossed the bridge.

"Who's that trip-trapping over my bridge?" roared the troll.

"It's only me!" said the middle-sized Billy Goat Gruff. "I'm going to eat the green grass on the other side of the bridge."

"Oh no, you're not!" roared the troll. "I'm going to eat you up!"

"But I'm just middle-sized," said the middle-sized Billy Goat Gruff. "Wait until the big goat comes across."

So the middle-sized Billy Goat Gruff crossed the bridge.

Next the big Billy Goat Gruff crossed the bridge.

"Who's that trip-trapping over my bridge?" roared the troll.

"It's only me!" said the big Billy Goat Gruff. "I'm going to eat the green grass on the other side of the bridge."

"Oh no, you're not!" roared the troll. "I'm going to eat you up!"

The troll jumped onto the bridge. The big Billy Goat Gruff lowered his horns.

Crash! Splash! The troll fell into the water.

The big Billy Goat Gruff skipped over the bridge and soon he was eating the green grass with the other Billy Goats Gruff.

And the bad troll was never seen again.

It's Raining, It's Pouring

It's raining, it's pouring,
The old man is snoring;
He went to bed and bumped his head
And couldn't get up in the morning.

Blow, Wind, Blow

Blow, wind, blow! And go, mill, go!
That the miller may grind his corn;
That the baker may take it,
And into rolls make it,
And send us some hot in the morn.

Rain, Rain, Go Away

Rain, rain,
Go away,
Come again
Another day.

Sneeze on Monday

Sneeze on Monday, sneeze for danger;
Sneeze on Tuesday, kiss a stranger;
Sneeze on Wednesday, get a letter;
Sneeze on Thursday, something better;
Sneeze on Friday, sneeze for sorrow;
Sneeze on Saturday, see your sweetheart tomorrow.

Jackanory

I'll tell you a story
Of Jackanory,
And now my story's begun;
I'll tell you another
Of Jack his brother,
And now my story's done.

Little Wind

Little wind, blow on the hill top;
Little wind, blow down the plain;
Little wind, blow up the sunshine;
Little wind, blow off the rain.

Troll Love

No one in Finn's village had been able to go anywhere for months. They were waiting for something, or someone, to save them from the troll. Their stores of food were almost gone—and they were scared.

Finally, Finn's father had had enough. "If we sneak out and go to the village on the other side of the mountain," he said to Finn, "we could muster enough people to scare off this terrible troll."

That night, Finn and his father set off. In the dead of night, they crept past the sleeping troll at the edge of the village. They were so close, they could smell his disgusting breath as he snored.

As dawn broke, they were halfway down the other side of the mountain, and they spied the other village not far below. But, to their horror, they saw a monstrous hairy troll pacing up and down at the edge of the village, thumping his chest with his fists.

"Oh no!" said Finn's father in alarm.

"I bet our troll wouldn't think much of another one being so close," said Finn, suddenly. "I bet they'd fight if they just happened to bump into each other."

"That's not a bad idea," said his father. "Why don't we make sure they do bump into each other?"

"*Hey!*" shouted Finn. "Big foot. Smelly breath. Up here!"
The troll stopped pacing and looked up with a grunt.

"This is it," cried Finn's father. "Run for your life!"

They turned and scrambled back up the mountain. The troll lumbered after them. As they approached their own village, the other troll turned to see what all the noise was about.

When the two trolls saw each other, they both let out a terrifying yell. Finn and his father hid behind a rock and waited for the battle to start.

But it didn't come. Finn peered out cautiously from his hiding place. The monsters were standing in front of each other and shuffling around nervously.

"What are they doing?" asked Finn.

"I don't know," whispered his father.

The two trolls sat down next to each other. Then, rather sheepishly, one reached out and took the other's hand. They stood there for a moment, then they started walking away into the woods together, murmuring gently as they went. Soon they were out of sight.

Finn and his father stared at each other in amazement.

"If I didn't know they were cruel, foul-smelling, people-eating monsters," said Finn's father, "I'd say those two have fallen in love."

And those two trolls never troubled the villages on the mountain again.

Monster Mash

Beware the monster mash!
'Cause monsters cook up trash,
Spaghetti hoops with liquorice loops—
They'll give you a nasty rash!

Beware the monster brew!
It's a grim and gristly stew,
Of turnip tops and vile black drops—
Not something you'd want to chew!

Beware the monster drink!
It's lime green, mauve, and pink,
And made with peas and dead gnats' knees—
It's bound to cause a stink!

Beware the monster gruel!
It's only good for fuel,
Brown rats' tails and slugs and snails—
To eat it would be cruel!

Beware the monster meat!
The special is dragons' feet,
With big curled claws and stinky paws—
They're gruesome, not a treat!

Beware the monster snack!
It's bubbling puce and black,
It's made from tar and bits of car—
So quickly hand it back!

And once you've had your fill,
Beware the monster bill,
If the food's not enough to make you rough—
The cost will make you ill!

Spectacular Slipup

An icy wind howled through the trees. Woozle the Wizard shivered and pulled his cloak tight against the whirling snow as he hurried home.

Whoomph! With a crash, Woozle collided with Mole, who was scurrying in the opposite direction.

While Mole picked up his glasses, Woozle straightened out his crumpled hat. Then they continued on their separate ways home.

Back at home, Woozle took down his spell book. He felt in his pocket for his reading glasses, but they weren't there.

"Oh, well, I'll just manage without," he said, turning the pages. "*Frog into Teapot*. I could use a new teapot!"

Peering closely at the words, he took a nice fat frog down from the shelf, waved his magic wand, and chanted the spell.

With a whoosh, the frog disappeared and in its place stood a tiny metal robot.

"Oh, dear," said Woozle. "I must have misread something."

Then he tried to turn a snail into toast, but got a ghost instead, and in place of a cake he got a garden rake.

Just then Woozle heard a scraping at the door. There, in a little frozen heap, lay Mole!

"What happened?" asked Woozle, helping Mole inside.

"I got lost," said Mole, through chattering teeth. "I've been wandering in the woods for hours trying to find my way home, but I couldn't see properly because my glasses were broken."

Just then, the ghost appeared. Mole jumped in fright. Woozle told Mole about his spells going wrong. "I need to find my reading glasses, but I don't know where to look," explained Woozle.

"Try your crystal ball," said Mole. "You can use my glasses—if you tape them up they should be OK."

Woozle put them on and blinked in amazement. "They're as good as my own!" he said. He gazed into his crystal ball. "I can see my glasses lying in the snow!" he said. "And here I am, bending down to pick them up—no, wait, it's not me, it's you!"

Woozle scratched his head, thinking hard. "I've got it!" he said. "My glasses must have fallen out of my pocket when we bumped into each other, and you picked them up by mistake. Which means your glasses are still in the snow, and my glasses are, well—they're right here on the end of my nose!"

Woozle changed the rake into cake and magicked Mole's glasses back onto his nose. The two friends tucked into a delicious snack, served up by the robot, who Woozle decided was much more useful than a teapot, and entertained by the ghost, who was very good at telling spooky stories.

Little Bunny

Come, little bunny,
Say, "Good night."
There's lots to do
Before you turn out the light.

Collect all your toys
And put them away.
Kiss them good night—
It's the end of the day.

Hop in the tub
For a rinse and a scrub.
Play with the bubbles—
Rub-a-dub-dub!

Finish your story
And turn out the light.
Time to tuck you in warmly
And kiss you good-night.

Mr. Moon

Look through the window
At the moon shining bright.
Who can you see
In the twinkling starlight?

Up in the trees,
The gray doves coo.
Calling a friendly
"Good night" to you.

Good night, little squirrel.
Good night, little mouse.
Hurrying, scurrying to bed
In the house.

Listen to Owl calling
"Who-whoo-whooo!"
While old Mr. Moon
Watches over you.

The Lost Boots

Ethan really wanted to get into the Space School powerball team. He had begged Mom to buy him some brand-new jet boots, and he practiced all weekend before the trials.

But on the morning of the trials, Ethan's new boots were not in his locker.

The old pair he borrowed were too big for him. During the trial's warm-up Ethan tripped and landed on his back. He knew he would never make the team.

Ethan limped off the court sadly, but Coach Cooper turned and stopped him.

"I know how much you want to be in this team, Ethan," he said. "So I'm going to make you a reserve. Don't worry, your time will come."

At the game Ethan sat on the bench, watching his team warm up.

"See how a real player does it," said Baz, the team captain. He fired a powerball straight at Ethan.

"Baz, I saw that," said Coach Cooper. "You're off my team."

"It's a stupid game, anyway!" shouted Baz. He stormed out,

kicking off his jet boots.

Ethan looked at the jet boots. They were just like his lost boots... in fact, they *were* his boots. Baz must have stolen them!

"Your turn, Ethan!" said Coach Cooper. Ethan couldn't believe his luck. He was in the powerball team.

The game began. Both teams were scoring well. Every player wanted to win. With a minute to go, Ethan's team were trailing by a point. Ethan switched his boots to turbo charge, and leaped into the air. He slammed the ball at the scoring plate, and it dropped neatly through the target.

The buzzer blew. Ethan's school team were the champions. Ethan had won the game!

"Well done, Ethan," said Coach Cooper. "We've never won the trophy before!"

Everyone cheered.

Take the Ghost Train

There's a tumbledown old station,
Where a ghost train waits to go.
All aboard, ghosts, ghouls, and goblins,
Watch the engine brightly glow!

Ghostly guards are whistling wildly,
Bony fingers wave good-bye,
As along the rails the ghost train glides,
Beneath the moonlit sky.

Witches shriek along the railcars,
While inside the dining car,
Vampires munch and crunch with monsters
Sipping cocktails at the bar!

If there were tickets for the ghost train,
Would you dare to take a ride?
Or would you quickly run away,
And find somewhere to hide?

Ode to Ghosts

A ghost he has a sad old life
Haunting empty castles.
On birthdays and at Christmas time
The mailman brings no parcels.

He floats around from room to room,
He howls and clanks his chains.
But everyone ignores the noise,
And blames it on the drains.

And if, by chance, he should appear
Most people scream with fright.
He just can't understand it—
Is he such a dreadful sight?

So if you ever meet a ghost
Don't run away in fright.
Stay awhile and talk a bit,
You'll find they're most polite.

Row, Row, Row Your Boat

Row, row, row your boat,
Gently down the stream,
Merrily, merrily, merrily, merrily,
Life is but a dream.

Jaybird

Jaybird, jaybird, sittin' on a rail,
Pickin' his teeth with the end of his tail;
Mulberry leaves and calico sleeves—
All school teachers are hard to please.

Spin, Dame

Spin, dame, spin,
Your bread you must win;
Twist the thread and break it not,
Spin, dame, spin.

The Robin and the Wren

The robin and the wren,
They fought upon the porridge pan;
But before the robin got a spoon,
The wren had eaten the porridge down.

The Mouse's Lullaby

Oh, rock-a-bye, baby mouse, rock-a-bye, so!
When baby's asleep to the baker's I'll go,
And while he's not looking I'll pop from a hole,
And bring to my baby a fresh penny roll.

Bow-wow

Bow-wow, says the dog,
Meow, meow, says the cat,
Grunt, grunt, goes the hog,
And squeak goes the rat.
Tu-whu, says the owl,
Caw, caw, says the crow,
Quack, quack, says the duck,
And what cuckoos say you know.

Short Shooter

Miss Travers clapped her hands. "We have two new students today," she said. "Daniel? Sophia? Come up here, please."

Daniel and his sister walked under the basketball hoop and across the wooden floor. They stood beside Miss Travers and looked at their new classmates. The class stared back.

"This is Daniel and Sophia Lutz," Miss Travers said. "They're twins."

Miss Travers turned to Sophia. "We have a few sports teams at Park Street Elementary School, Sophia. What's your favorite sport?" she asked.

"Soccer," Sophia said right away.

A couple of girls in the front row smiled and gave her a "thumbs up" sign.

"And how about you, Daniel?" Miss Travers asked.

Daniel held his breath. He looked at the hoop above his head. He'd give anything to play on the school team.

"I like basketball," he mumbled.

Miss Travers nodded, but quiet laughter and whispers came from some

of the class.

"You're too short for basketball!" a boy called.

Daniel's face felt hot.

"He's not!" Sophia said, defending her brother. "He practices with our big brother Mark all the time!"

Miss Travers turned to the boy who'd called out. "Get the ball bag please, Jason," she said. "We're playing basketball today."

The familiar sound of bouncing balls made Daniel feel calm. He stood in line with the others, shooting at the basket when it was his turn. Balls escaped into every corner of the room, but Daniel never missed a shot.

Miss Travers blew a whistle. "Jason and Daniel, come here please."

The two boys stood beside each other in front of the coach. Daniel was a head shorter than Jason.

"I've been watching you, Daniel," Miss Travers said. "I need another player for the basketball team." She bounced the ball to him. "If you can get a basket past Jason, you're on the team."

Jason laughed. "Ready, shorty?" he said. He spread his arms.

The class was silent as Daniel stood on his toes to peer over the taller boy's shoulder. The basket looked far away. He took a deep breath.

"If you can beat Mark, you can beat Jason!" Sophia yelled.

Jason waved his arms. "Come on, shorty, move!"

Daniel did.

He dribbled the ball and ducked under Jason's arm. He raced toward the basket, but Jason leaped in front of him. Keeping his body between Jason and the ball, Daniel turned his back on the taller boy. He sped away from the basket.

His mind moved faster than his feet as Daniel worked out a plan. Mark had taught him a new move. It just might work. Could he do it?

As he reached center court, Daniel slowed. His muscles were tense as the footsteps behind him grew faster and closer. When it sounded like Jason was in a full sprint, Daniel stepped to the side and spun around. He raced toward his basket.

"Hey!" Jason shouted from behind.

Daniel threw the ball as Jason skidded to a stop beside him. They both watched the ball sail toward the net. It hit the rim once, twice, and then a third time before it dropped through the hoop and hit the floor.

"Do you still think he's too short, Jason?" someone yelled.

Jason picked up the ball and handed it to Daniel. "Welcome to the team," he said with a grin.

Fall Fires

In the other yards
And all up the vale,
From the fall bonfires,
See the smoke trail!

Pleasant summer over
And all the summer flowers,
The red fire blazes,
The gray smoke towers.

Sing a song of seasons!
Something bright in all!
Flowers in the summer,
Fires in the fall!

If All the Oceans Were One Ocean

If all the oceans were one ocean,
What a great ocean that would be!
And if all the trees were one tree,
What a great tree that would be!
And if all the axes were one ax,
What a great ax that would be!
And if all the men were one man,
What a great man that would be!
And if the great man took the great ax,
And cut down the great tree,
And let it fall in the great ocean,
What a splish splash that would be!

Snap! Snap!

One quiet, lazy morning, Claudia Crocodile was drifting down the river looking for fun. In the distance, she could see Mickey and Madison Monkey playing on the riverbank.

"I'll give them a fright," decided Claudia. "It's always amusing to watch them run away!"

Sure enough, the *Snap! Snap!* of Claudia's strong jaws scared the little monkeys.

That afternoon, Claudia was feeling bored again, so she looked for someone else to frighten.

She saw Timmy Tiger on his own and crept up right behind him! *Snap! Snap!* went her great big jaws.

He was trembling with terror. But Claudia didn't eat him, as he thought she would.

"Why haven't you eaten me?" asked Timmy timidly.

"I don't want to eat you. You're furry and yucky! I only *Snap!* to scare people. That's what crocodiles are supposed to do."

"I never knew you could be nice. I like you! I think everyone would like you," said Timmy, "if you could just be friendly, instead of scary."

As Timmy and Claudia went along together, they saw Mickey and Madison trying to smash open some coconuts.

"Here's your chance," Timmy told Claudia.

Claudia nodded and swam toward the monkeys, *Snap! Snap! Snapping!* As soon as they heard her, the monkeys ran.

"It's all right," said Claudia, "I just want to help. Throw me a coconut!"

The monkeys were uncertain, but Mickey tossed his coconut at Claudia's gaping jaws. *Snap! Snap! Snap!*

Quick as a flash, the coconut was open.

"Gosh, Claudia, thanks!" said an amazed Mickey.

Claudia opened Madison's coconut, too.

Soon, everyone was happy sharing the cool, refreshing milk and chomping on chewy chunks of coconut.

But happiest of all was Claudia, who had found that having friends was so much more fun than scaring them!

Mythical Monster

The monster lay in the mud at the bottom of Green Lake. She was sad. Everything had changed. Once, she'd been the most famous monster in the world. But now only a few people bothered to stand around on the shore waiting for a glimpse of her.

The monster knew what had gone wrong—she'd made too few appearances. Once every twenty years just wasn't enough. People had gotten bored waiting.

She knew what to do. She had to make a splash! She swam across the lake, her spotted back breaking the surface. But when she lifted her neck, she saw that the shore was empty. In the distance there was a campsite, but the people there weren't looking toward the lake. They were outside their tents, reading newspapers and cooking dinner. No one was interested in her.

She'd have to show herself properly, she decided. She swam to the shore and lumbered into the middle of the campsite.

A woman walked out of a tent. "Hey kids, that's a great costume," she cried when she saw the monster. "Wherever did you get it? Now wash up. Dinner'll be ready in just a few minutes."

As the monster was walking sadly back to the lake, a boy came

along. He screamed. "It's the Green Lake Monster!" he shouted.

"I wouldn't bother yourself with all that," said the monster to the astonished boy. "No one believes in me anymore."

"That's terrible," said the boy. "We'll have to think of something that will get people's attention. I know—why don't I row out onto the lake and then pretend to be in trouble. Then you can rescue me."

The boy rowed himself out onto the lake, then deliberately pushed the oars away. "Help! I'm going to drown!" he cried.

The campers came running to the shore. Right on cue, the monster reared up out of the water. A great wave engulfed the boat, tossing the boy into the water.

"The monster's attacking my son!" cried a woman.

"That isn't what I had in mind," thought the monster. She plucked the boy from the water with her huge jaws.

"It's eating my son!" cried the woman.

Holding the boy in her mouth, the monster swam to the shore and put him down in front of his mother.

"The monster's saved my son!" cried the woman. "It's a hero!"

Cameras were flashing everywhere. "That's enough for me," the monster thought. She dived to the bottom of the lake. "I'll lay low for a while," she said to herself. "Just for another twenty years or so. A monster can only take so much attention, after all."

There Was an Old Man With a Beard

There was an old man with a beard,
Who said, "It is just as I feared!—
Two owls and a hen, four larks and a wren
Have all built their nests in my beard!"

Greedy Tom

Jimmy the Mowdy
Made a great crowdy;
Barney O'Neal
Found all the meal;
Old Jack Rutter
Sent two stone of butter;
The Laird of the Hot
Boiled it in his pot;
And Big Tom of the Hall
He supped it all.

Punctuality

Be always in time,
Too late is a crime.

Here's the Lady's Knives and Forks

Here's the lady's knives and forks.
Here's the lady's table.
Here's the lady's looking glass.
And here's the baby's cradle.
Rock! Rock! Rock! Rock!

On Oath

As I went to Bonner,
I met a pig
Without a wig,
Upon my word and honor.

Bless You

Bless you, bless you, burnie-bee,
Tell me when my wedding be;
If it be tomorrow day,
Take your wings and fly away.
Fly to the east, fly to the west,
Fly to him I love the best.

Muddy Puddle

It was a sunny day on the farm. The animals were hot and thirsty. Farmer Fred whistled cheerily as he carried his bucket to the water faucet. Farmer Fred turned on the faucet. It whistled and clanked, but no water came out. He turned on every faucet in the farmyard, but not a drop of water came out.

"I don't believe it, there's no water!" he cried.

Meanwhile, Patch the sheepdog set off to check on the sheep. But as he passed Hog Hollow, he heard a grunting noise.

"My muddy puddle has dried up," Polly Pig complained. "If I don't get a mud bath soon, I'm sure to get sunburned."

"I'll fetch Farmer Fred," barked Patch. "He'll think of something."

"Trembling tomatoes!" cried Farmer Fred when he saw Polly Pig. "We need to make a mud bath. But there's no water in the faucets."

Just then, he heard Dotty Duck quacking.

"I have an idea!" said Farmer Fred.

Farmer Fred fetched two buckets of water from the brook and carried them back to Hog Hollow. He tipped them into Polly's dried-up muddy patch, and then went to fetch more.

Up and down, up and down he went. But when he stopped for a rest, he couldn't believe his eyes. Hog Hollow was as dry as ever!

"Brilliant buckets! It's drying up faster than I can fill it!" cried Farmer Fred.

"Well, perhaps Harry Horse can help," thought Farmer Fred. But when Farmer Fred attached two buckets over Harry's back, Harry simply dug in his hoofs and refused to budge.

"Neigh! Neigh!" he complained. It was far too hot to work.

"Oh, dear," said Farmer Fred, fanning Polly with his hat. "How are we going to make you a mud bath?"

Just then, he spotted a length of hose curled up beside the milking parlor.

"Never fear!" he cried, "I have an idea!" And, grabbing the hose, he raced back to his workshop.

Farmer Fred crashed around inside his workshop. Before long, the door swung open. The animals stood back as Farmer Fred pushed out a machine with the hose attached.

"This," explained Farmer Fred, "is a pump-action, sun-powered Puddle Filler. We'll soon have the biggest mud bath you have ever seen."

"Whatever is he up to now?" neighed Harry Horse, shaking his head. Everyone held their breath as Farmer Fred flipped a switch on the Puddle Filler. It spluttered into life.

"Now, just wait for the water," cried Farmer Fred.

Suddenly, the hose began to hiss and squirm.

"Popping parsnips!" cried Farmer Fred, as the Puddle Filler reared up and chased him around Hog Hollow.

Everyone scattered as it snaked and flapped this way and that.

Farmer Fred landed with a bump next to Polly Pig.

"It doesn't look like you'll be getting your mud bath after all!" he said. Then Farmer Fred felt a drip fall on his head.

"Hurray, it's raining!" he cried.

"Woof, woof," barked Patch, looking up at the tree above the pigpen. Farmer Fred looked up. It wasn't raining. The hose was stuck in the tree and a cool shower was falling over Hog Hollow.

Just then, Jenny appeared at Hog Hollow with some good news.

"The water company said there was a burst pipe. It's fixed now, so the faucets should be working."

At that moment, water gushed out of the faucets in the farmyard. Before long, Polly, Patch, and the other animals were jumping in all the muddy puddles.

"It never rains but it pours," laughed Farmer Fred.

Smoky Smells Success

Smoky was a spook who haunted an ancient castle. And, being a ghost, Smoky could change shape at will.

"What should I be next?" the spook wondered. "Headless the Horrible or Sir Percy, the Chain-Dragging Prisoner?" Smoky just loved inventing new spooky disguises. He only wished he had more visitors to try them out on.

One morning, Smoky heard a car pull up. A man and woman climbed out. They walked slowly around the castle walls, making notes, and looking very serious indeed.

"It's no use," said the man. "The castle's crumbling. We'll have to forget opening it to the public."

"If only we could raise enough money to repair it," replied the woman.

Smoky froze. If his castle was pulled down, what would happen to him? Something had to be done!

As the visitors were returning to their car, they suddenly stopped and sniffed the air. There was a wonderful smell coming from the castle. The man pointed to what looked like a thin trail of steam floating by the entrance. It was Smoky, who had conjured up a delicious smell to tempt the visitors in.

Smoky led the man and the woman through the castle,

disguised as the thin trail of smoke. A secret door mysteriously swung open, and a narrow, cobweb-filled passage led the visitors to a hidden chamber and... a treasure chest!

"Unbelievable! There's more than enough money here to rebuild the castle ten times," cried the man.

Then the visitors shivered and glanced uneasily around.

"What about the ghosts people say live here?" said the man.

"Maybe they're friendly ghosts," said the woman. "But let's not stick around to find out!"

Soon after, workmen arrived to restore the castle. At first, they were nervous—but Smoky stayed out of sight.

The day before the castle was finally opened, the mayor came to look around. "It's such a pity the castle doesn't seem to be haunted after all," he said. "That would really put it on the map."

You can guess who was listening! Smoky chuckled with glee. He was more than happy to oblige! Quick as a flash he appeared as a court jester, then disappeared through the wall. The mayor almost jumped out of his skin!

After that Smoky had a wonderful time, trying out all his disguises on visitors who trembled with excitement as they searched the castle for ghosts. After all, everyone likes being a little bit scared now and then—don't you?

Hippo Stays Awake

It was a *very* hot day in the jungle.

"It's too warm to do anything except snooze," thought Hatty Hippo, and she lay down by the waterhole.

Suddenly, the ground began to shake. *Thud, thud, thud!*

"It's only me!" trumpeted Effie Elephant. "I've just come for a quick shower to cool myself down."

Effie stood in the waterhole and sprayed water all over her back. *Slop! Slosh!*

The air was suddenly filled with loud cries.

"*Wheeee!*" It was a troop of monkeys swinging through the trees. "Anyone for a water fight?" they called loudly.

"*Squawk, squawk!* Yes please!" the parrots shrieked.
Splosh! Splash! Whee! Squawk!

Hatty groaned. How would she ever get to sleep now?

"*Quiet!*" yelled Hatty, louder than any of the other animals. All the noise stopped at once.

"Sorry, Hatty," whispered Effie. "You only had to say something." One by one, the animals tiptoed away.

Finally, the jungle was silent. "Aaaahh!" yawned Hatty, settling down. "Now I'm on my own, I'll get a little bit of peace at last!"

The Big Blue Egg

One morning, Little Brown Hen found a strange thing in
the farmyard. It was big, blue, and round. Little Brown Hen
walked slowly around the big blue thing. She sniffed it, tapped
it with her beak, and listened.

"Well, it's round like an egg," she said. "So it must be an
egg. I'll keep it warm until it hatches."

Little Brown Hen settled down to wait for the egg to
hatch. She waited… and waited… and waited… but nothing
happened.

"Perhaps it isn't warm enough," she worried, giving the egg
a nudge with her beak. Oops! The big blue egg toppled out of
the nest and began to bounce away.

Boing! Boing! Boing! The egg bounced across the farmyard.
"Stop that egg!" cried Little Brown Hen, running after it as
fast as she could.

Up jumped Sheeba the sheepdog. She caught the runaway
egg between her paws.

"I've been looking for this all day,"
barked Sheeba. "Thank you for finding
it for me!"

"I didn't know that dogs laid eggs!"
said Little Brown Hen.

"It's not an egg, silly," laughed
Sheeba. "It's my puppy's favorite
bouncy ball!"

The Planet Where Time Goes Backward

Far beyond our solar system,
In the outer reaches of space,
There's a planet where time goes backward,
And it's the most peculiar place.

Cooks wash the dishes before the meal starts,
And unpeel potatoes, I'm told.
Your dinner goes into the oven
And comes out nice and cold.

Gas pumps take the gas out of cars,
And soccer's not much of a laugh:
The game ends with both teams at zero,
And they start by taking a bath.

You know something bad's going to happen,
When somebody starts to cry.
But the people get younger each day,
And they greet you by saying "Good-bye!"

A Whale of a Time

Did you hear the story of Wendy Bligh?
The remarkable whale who loved to fly?
It happened like this. She was sleeping one day,
When a hot-air balloonist flew her way.
He looked down below and spotted her hump,
"I'll land on that rock," said he, with a thump.
He tied up his balloon with a beautiful bow,
While Wendy slept on—she just didn't know.
Then a big tornado whirled over the ocean,
It blew Wendy upward with a huge swirling motion.
"What a wonderful feeling!" the whale cried in glee.
"The whole sparkling ocean is lying beneath me!"
The hot-air balloonist took her for a spin,
She chatted to birds and waved her huge fin.
He dropped her back home at the end of the day.
"Oh thank you!" she smiled, and then swam away.

Teamwork

"Hey, Sophia! Ready for your first game?" called Brittany, captain of the Park Street Elementary School Girls' Soccer Team.

Sophia finished her sit-ups and stood up. "I think so," she said. "What's the Oakfield Elementary team like?"

"They're one of the best," Brittany replied. "It's going to be a good game!"

Sophia glanced around. A lot of people had come to watch! Her stomach jumped and her palms felt damp.

"Hey, Sophia!" a voice called from the side.

Sophia spotted her brother. She smiled and waved. Just knowing Daniel was there made her feel better. She jogged onto the field and took her position.

"Let's go for it, Park Street!" called Brittany.

Miss Travers placed the ball on the center line and stood back. Park Street was kicking off first.

Brittany raced up to the ball and kicked it to Jackie. The game was on!

The ball was a blur as it was dribbled and passed from one girl to another. Sophia forgot to be nervous as she played the game she loved best.

"Ana!" Sophia passed the ball and watched Ana shoot it past the goalie and into the net.

Miss Travers raised both arms overhead. "Goal!" she shouted.

The first half of the game flew by. Sophia kicked, blocked, and defended. She was always in the right place to pass to the girl who scored.

By the end of the first half, Park Street Elementary was ahead by one goal. The score was 3-2.

Sophia waved to Daniel as she ran onto the field for the second half of the game. She was glad he was watching. She just wished she could score a goal. Then she'd really feel like a part of the team.

The game continued. Oakfield Elementary scored another goal so the score was an even 3-3. With only five minutes left, it was Park Street's turn to kick off.

Sophia wiped her face and hands on her shirt. They needed one more goal.

Would they be able to do it?

Brittany kicked the ball and Ana raced after it. She was fast, but not fast enough! A forward from Oakfield stole the ball and dribbled down the field.

Sophia sprinted after the forward. Her feet pounded into the grass. The forward's ponytail swished just out of reach. Sophia pushed her legs harder. She edged past and touched the ball with her toe. It spun to the side where Ana was ready.

Ana dribbled the ball back toward the Oakfield goal. Sophia raced down the pitch after her.

"Sophia!" Ana passed the ball to Sophia. Sophia dribbled it for a few steps but wasn't close enough to make a shot. She looked for a teammate who was clear.

"It's yours, Brittany!" Sophia kicked the ball toward the team captain and Brittany flicked it into the goal.

"Goal!" Miss Travers shouted. "Park Street wins!"

Sophia ran to help the team lift Brittany onto their shoulders. But then she stopped. The rest of the team were now running toward her!

"What are you doing?" Sophia asked, as the girls crowded around her, smiling.

"It takes more than one person to score a goal, Sophia," Brittany said, as she and the rest of the team lifted Sophia into the air. "You helped to score them all!"

93

Brother and Sister

"*Sister*, sister, go to bed!
Go and rest your weary head."
Thus the prudent brother said.

"Do you want a battered hide,
Or scratches to your face applied?"
Thus his sister calm replied.

"Sister, do not raise my wrath.
I'd make you into mutton broth
As easily as kill a moth!"

The sister raised her beaming eye
And looked on him indignantly
And sternly answered, "Only try!"

Off to the cook he quickly ran.
"Dear Cook, please lend a frying pan
To me as quickly as you can."

"And wherefore should I lend it you?"
"The reason, Cook, is plain to view.
I wish to make an Irish stew."

"What meat is in that stew to go?"
"My sister'll be the contents!" "Oh!"
"You'll lend the pan to me, Cook?" "No!"

Moral: Never stew your sister.

A Rat

There was a rat,
For want of stairs,
Went down a rope
To say his prayers.

Diddelty, Diddelty

Diddlety, diddlety, dumpty,
The cat ran up the plum tree;
Half a crown to fetch her down,
Diddlety, diddlety, dumpty.

Milking

Let down thy milk, old brown cow,
Let down thy milk and I'll give you a bow;
A bow, a coin, and a golden key,
If thou wilt make sweet white milk for me.

Little Jack Jingle

Little Jack Jingle,
He used to live single;
But when he got tired of this kind of life,
He quit being single, and lived with his wife.

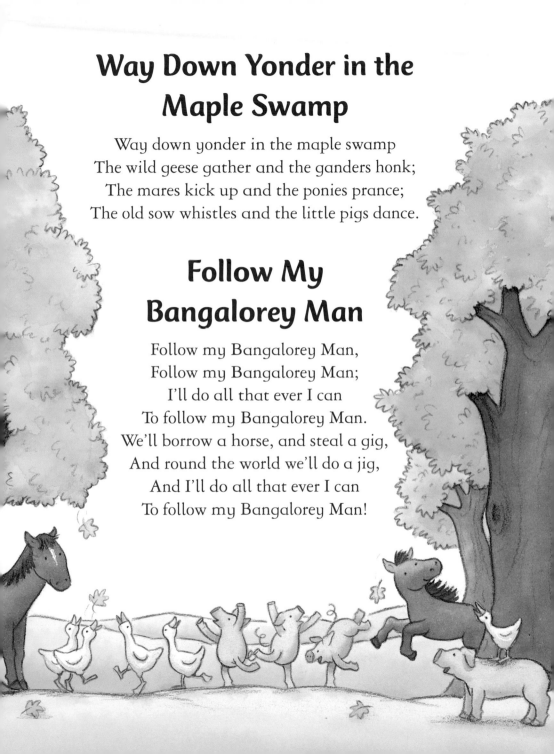

Way Down Yonder in the Maple Swamp

Way down yonder in the maple swamp
The wild geese gather and the ganders honk;
The mares kick up and the ponies prance;
The old sow whistles and the little pigs dance.

Follow My Bangalorey Man

Follow my Bangalorey Man,
Follow my Bangalorey Man;
I'll do all that ever I can
To follow my Bangalorey Man.
We'll borrow a horse, and steal a gig,
And round the world we'll do a jig,
And I'll do all that ever I can
To follow my Bangalorey Man!

The Spooks' Ball

At midnight they gather. They are off to a ball,
Which is held once a year in the Haunted Hall.
There they all dance by the light of the moon,
While the spooky band plays a terrible tune.

A vampire violinist stabs out notes with her bow,
There's a skull for a drum, and a piano
That's made from the teeth of a dinosaur.
The skeletons dance and call out for more!

There's a ghost with his head tucked under his arm.
He feeds it with chips without causing alarm.
A witch and her cat are dancing a jig.
But the witch can't keep up 'cause her boots are too big.

But the time will soon come for the sun to rise,
And the spooks will all vanish before your eyes.
They've had such frightful fun at the ball tonight,
Will you see them next year? Well you just might…

The Toast Ghost

A hungry ghost wished for some toast.
"I'd eat a loaf!" he'd often boast.
The words he longed someone to utter
Were, "Here's hot toast with lots of butter!"

The ghost despaired. "What should I do?"
A mouse replied, "If I were you,
I'd seek a café or a restaurant.
Ask them to make the toast you want!"

So he found a café, and a kitchen.
For buttered toast the ghost was itchin'!
Then something white behind the door
Floated softly to the floor.

The nervous ghost took off in fright.
He found he'd lost his appetite.
"I couldn't even eat a pea!"
But let me tell, 'tween you and me...

It was the chef's white hat he saw.
That ghost, he don't eat toast no more!

Jack and the Beanstalk

Once upon a time there was a boy named Jack. He lived with his mother in a cottage. They were very poor.

One day, Jack's mother said, "We have no food left to eat and no money to buy it with. Take the cow to market and sell her."

So Jack took the cow to market. On the way, Jack met a very old man walking along the road.

"Where are you going?" asked the old man.

"I am going to market to sell the cow," said Jack.

The old man offered Jack five magic beans for the cow. Jack agreed and sold the cow, then took the beans home.

"I sold the cow for five magic beans," he told his mother.

"Five beans!" she said. She was cross! She threw the magic beans out of the window.

Then she sent Jack to bed without any supper.

In the morning, Jack woke up. He looked out of the window. There was a giant beanstalk. It went up, up into the sky.

Jack climbed up the beanstalk.

At the top, there was a giant castle. Jack knocked on the door. The door opened.

Jack went in. Everything in the castle was enormous. That was because a giant and his wife lived in the castle.

"Fee, fi, fo, fum!" said the giant. "I want my breakfast."
Jack was afraid.

"You must hide," said the giant's wife, "or my husband will
eat you."

Jack hid from the giant.

The giant sat down at the table. Then he
put a hen on the table.

"Hen, lay an egg!" said the giant. The
hen laid a golden egg.

"Here is your breakfast," said the
giant's wife.

His wife gave him a very big breakfast.

The giant ate his breakfast. Then he felt
very sleepy. "Time for my nap," he said.

Soon he was fast asleep.

"A golden egg!" said Jack. "I will take the hen.
She will lay golden eggs and make us rich."

"Cluck!" said the hen. The giant woke up! Jack
ran to the beanstalk. The giant ran after him.

But Jack got his ax and chopped down
the beanstalk.

When the beanstalk fell to the ground,
the giant came crashing down with it.
That was the end of him!

Then the hen laid a golden egg.

And soon Jack and his mother weren't poor
anymore!

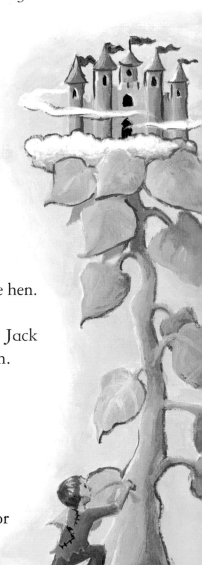

Helpful Little Digger

Little Yellow Digger was very excited. It was his first day on the building site.

Chug! Chug! Chug!

Bulldozer was hard at work, pushing piles of dirt.

"Please may I help you?" asked Little Yellow Digger.

"I don't need any help, thanks," replied Bulldozer. "Now watch out, or you'll get knocked over!"

Dump Truck was working nearby. "I don't need any help either, Little Yellow Digger," he called.

Beep! Beep! Beep! Dump Truck's back lifted up.

"I'd better get out of the way quickly, before I'm buried in sand," thought Little Yellow Digger. He felt very unhappy. "Nobody wants my help on this site," he sighed.

Then Bulldozer and Dump Truck went *splutter* and *cough*. "We've been working too hard!" they gasped. "We're running out of fuel!"

"I'll help," cried Little Yellow Digger, and he sped toward a pile of fuel drums. Little Yellow Digger took drums of fuel to his two friends. Soon they were working again.

"You were good at helping after all," they cheered. "Hooray for Little Yellow Digger!"

The Incredible Centipede

I'm not just an ordinary centipede,
I live in a circus van.
I know all the top performers,
And I have a wonderful plan...

We'll reach a town, and as the sun goes down,
The folks will crowd the tent;
With music to thrill, they'll look at the lineup
And read with astonishment:

"Star of the show in the ring tonight,
And we hope he does succeed,
Is the enterprising, most surprising,
Incredible Centipede!"

The curtains will part and out I'll dart
And shake a leg or six,
Then in spangled tights I'll scale the heights
To perform my amazing tricks.

It will be so grand, in every land,
Royalty will want to be seen
Meeting the Incredible Centipede—
And I'll meet lots of kings and queens.

Seesaw, Sacradown

Seesaw, Sacradown,
Which is the way to London Town?
One foot up and one foot down,
That's the way to London Town.

Over the Hills and Far Away

When I was young and had no sense,
I bought a fiddle for eighteen cents,
And the only tune that I could play
Was, "Over the Hills and Far Away."

As I Was Going Along

As I was going along, long, long,
A-singing a comical song, song, song,
The lane that I went on was so long, long, long,
And the song that I sang was as long, long, long,
And so I went singing along.

A Sailor Went to Sea

A sailor went to sea, sea, sea,
To see what he could see, see, see,
But all that he could see, see, see,
Was the bottom of the deep blue sea, sea, sea.

From Wibbleton to Wobbleton

From Wibbleton to Wobbleton is fifteen miles,
From Wobbleton to Wibbleton is fifteen miles,
From Wibbleton to Wobbleton,
From Wobbleton to Wibbleton,
From Wibbleton to Wobbleton is fifteen miles.

One, Two, Three, Four, Five

One, two, three, four, five,
Once I caught a fish alive;
Six, seven, eight, nine, ten,
Then I let him go again.
Why did you let him go?
Because he bit my finger so.
Which finger did he bite?
This little finger on the right.

Farmer Fred's Worried Hen

It was an icy cold day and Farmer Fred had just finished milking the cows.

Suddenly, the door swung open and Farmer Fred's wife, Jenny, burst in.

"Hetty Hen has hatched twelve chicks," panted Jenny. "There's just one egg left to hatch."

Farmer Fred and his dog, Patch, ran over to the hen house to check on Hetty Hen's progress.

There were twelve fluffy new chicks huddling together. Hetty Hen was still keeping the thirteenth egg warm.

"What's happening?" Patch asked the other animals.

"Sssshhh!" whispered Polly Pig. "Hetty's concentrating."

"It's just too cold in this hen house," clucked Hetty Hen. "This egg is never going to hatch."

"Never fear, I've got an idea!" Farmer Fred cried. Then he disappeared into his workshop.

After a lot of banging and crashing, the door to the workshop swung open and out stepped Farmer Fred. He was carrying a see-through box in his arms with a light bulb inside.

"This," Farmer Fred declared, "is a Super-heated Egg Hatcher." He put the egg into the Super-heated Egg Hatcher.

Everyone sat back and waited. Suddenly, there was a pop and a fizz and the lightbulb flickered out.

"Never fear!" said Farmer Fred. "It just needs a new lightbulb." And off he went to the farmhouse.

"Woof!" barked Patch, wagging his tail. He had a great idea. Patch followed Farmer Fred into the farmhouse, picked up Farmer Fred's cap, and put it gently beside the fire.

Farmer Fred looked at his cap beside the fire.

"That's it!" he cried, grabbing his hat. Farmer Fred dashed outside and came back with the unhatched egg in his cap. Hetty Hen and the other animals followed him into the house.

"There," said Farmer Fred, laying the cap and egg beside the fire.

Everyone sat back and waited. Just then, *Crack!* The egg began to hatch... and out popped the thirteenth chick.

"Cheep! Cheep!" chirped the chick, hopping onto Farmer Fred's lap.

"I always knew this was the warmest place on the farm for hatching eggs," smiled Farmer Fred.

"Woof, woof!" barked Patch.

Chicken Licken

One day, Chicken Licken was scratching for food in the woods when, *Boink!* an acorn fell onto her head.

"Ruffle my feathers!" said Chicken Licken. "The sky is falling down. I must tell the king at once." And off she ran as fast she could.

On her way, Chicken Licken met Cocky Locky.

"I'm off to tell the king that the sky's falling down!" Chicken Licken said.

"Goodness!" clucked Cocky Locky. "I'd better come with you." And off they hurried.

On their way to see the king, Chicken Licken and Cocky Locky met Ducky Lucky.

"We're off to tell the king that the sky's falling down!" Chicken Licken said.

"Babbling brooks!" quacked Ducky Lucky. "Let's go. There's no time to lose."

They had just set off again, when they saw Goosey Loosey.

"We're off to tell the king the sky is falling down!" Chicken Licken said.

Goosey Loosey was very worried. "I'd better come, too," she honked. So the four birds went along, until they met Foxy Loxy.

"Good day to you all!" said the crafty fox. "Where are you

going this fine day?"

Chicken Licken puffed up her chest importantly. "We're off to see the king," she announced. "The sky fell on my head in the woods. We must tell him at once."

Foxy Loxy grinned slyly. "Let me show you the quickest way there," he said, leading the way.

So Chicken Licken, Cocky Locky, Ducky Lucky, and Goosey Loosey all followed Foxy Loxy until they came to a narrow, dark hole in the hillside.

"Follow me!" said sly Foxy Loxy. With that, he led Goosey Loosey, Ducky Lucky, and Cocky Locky into his den. Chicken Licken was about to follow when all of a sudden there was a terrible honking and quacking and crowing from the hole!

"Oh no!" cried Chicken Licken. "Foxy Loxy has eaten Goosey Loosey, Ducky Lucky, and Cocky Locky!"

She ran as fast as she could away from Foxy Loxy's den.

And Chicken Licken never did get to tell the king that the sky was falling down.

Ethan's Birthday

Ethan woke up early. He had been waiting for this day for weeks, and now it was here at last. It was his birthday!

Ethan couldn't wait to open all his presents. He hoped one of them was the latest album by Alan and the Aliens, his favorite band.

He jumped out of bed and ran downstairs. Mom was in the kitchen oiling Tina the House Robot.

"Hello, Ethan," said Mom. "Could you lay the breakfast table, please? Tina's not working this morning."

Ethan couldn't believe his ears. No "Happy Birthday?"

"Where's Dad?" he asked.

"He's gone to work," said Mom. "He had to leave early because he's got a busy day."

Zelda ran into the kitchen. "I've got a school trip today!" she said. "My teacher told us to get to school early, because the space bus leaves at eight o'clock."

"We'd better rush!" said Mom. She handed Ethan a carton of milk. "Get your own breakfast, Ethan," she said. "I've got to take Zelda to school."

They had all forgotten his birthday!

Things didn't get better at Space School. Ethan had all his worst lessons.

At home time, Ethan's best friend Spud tried to cheer him up. "I'll race you!" he said. They bounced home on their space hoppers.

When Ethan got home, Dad opened the front door.

"Surprise!" he said. All Ethan's family were there, waiting to see him. There were balloons everywhere, and there was a huge pile of presents.

"We didn't really forget," said Mom, giving Ethan a kiss. "Go on, birthday boy, open your presents!"

Ethan ripped open an envelope. He thought it was probably just a card from Aunt Alice, who lived on Mars.

"It's tickets to see Alan and the Aliens at the Moondust Superdrome tonight!" he cried.

"We're all going— Spud, too," said Dad.

Ethan grinned. It looked like this was going to be a fantastic birthday after all!

The Nasty Nice Spell

Of all the goblins that have ever played tricks upon the human world, Gordon Grizzle was surely the most cunning, mean, and spiteful of them all. Every day, he crept around watching and waiting until he got the chance to spoil a person's happiness.

"That Gordon Grizzle will go too far one day!" warned Marcus Mildew, who was a very wise old goblin. The other goblins nodded and scratched their scruffy beards thoughtfully.

"But what can we do?" Marcus continued. "Aha! I think I might have an idea," he said, mysteriously.

The next day, when Gordon was snooping around looking for something really nasty to do, he overheard a conversation between two women.

"Young Ashley's marrying Fred today," one of them was saying. "She's made a beautiful wedding gown. Of course, she had to make it from scraps of fabric, being so poor."

Gordon didn't hear the other woman's reply, because he was already scheming. He knew perfectly well why Ashley was so poor. Why, wasn't it he himself who had

turned her father's lottery winnings into
fall leaves and floated them down the
river? Gordon grinned to himself—well,
here's a chance to have some fun,
he thought.

He could hear the wedding bells ringing
and scampered off to the church, just in time
to see Ashley arrive. Gordon had to admit
that she did look lovely in her pretty white dress.
"Not for long!" he thought spitefully, as he cast his spell:
  "Eye of bat and tooth of hag,
  Make Ashley's gown a tattered rag!"
Bam! The deed was done. Gordon giggled to himself. He
heard the wedding guests gasp as they looked at Ashley.
"I bet she looks truly awful," he giggled to himself. But then he
peeped out from behind a pew, and to his utter astonishment,
there was Ashley wearing the most gorgeous silver
gown he'd ever seen.

"That'll teach you!" said a familiar
voice from behind him. It was Marcus
Mildew. "I've been watching you,
Gordon," he said. "I've seen your
spiteful ways, spoiling everyone's
fun. So I decided to spoil your fun,
too! From now on, every time you
cast a spell you'll find the opposite
happens!"

Three Young Rats

Three young rats with black felt hats,
Three young ducks with white straw flats,
Three young dogs with curling tails,
Three young cats with demi-veils,
Went out to walk with two young pigs
In satin vests and sorrel wigs;
But suddenly it chanced to rain,
And so they all went home again.

Humpty Dumpty

Humpty Dumpty sat on a wall,
Humpty Dumpty had a great fall;
All the king's horses and all the king's men
Couldn't put Humpty together again.

We're All in the Dumps

We're all in the dumps,
For diamonds and trumps,
The kittens are gone to St. Paul's,
The babies are bit,
The moon's in a fit,
And the houses are built without walls.

Tweedle-dum and Tweedle-dee

Tweedle-dum and Tweedle-dee
Agreed to have a battle,
For Tweedle-dum said Tweedle-dee
Had spoiled his nice new rattle.
Just then flew down a monstrous crow,
As big as a tar barrel,
Which frightened both the heroes so,
They quite forgot their quarrel.

Daffy-Down-Dilly

Daffy-Down-Dilly
Has come up to town
In a yellow petticoat
And a green gown.

Little Tommy Tittlemouse

Little Tommy Tittlemouse
Lived in a little house;
He caught fishes
In other men's ditches.

Fiddlefingers

Captain Brassbuttons hummed happily and tapped his feet to a lively tune on board his pirate ship, *The Jolly Jig*.

The crew of *The Jolly Jig* preferred making music and having a merry time to pirating. After all, raiding ships was hard and dangerous work.

"'Tis a pity we don't have a fiddle player among us, cap'n," said Jake one day.

As he said this, a strong current suddenly picked the pirate ship up and whirled it away. When the ship finally came to rest, a wreck was drifting alongside the pirates.

"Stand by to board!" Brassbuttons cried to his men.

As Brassbuttons entered the crew's quarters of the wreck, he heard a terrible noise coming from a dark corner.

"Who goes there?" he called. Then, to his surprise, he saw a sailor lying in a hammock, snoring. There was a fiddle resting on the sailor's chest.

Brassbuttons poked the sailor with his cutlass and he woke with a start. "Who are you?" he gasped.

"We might ask the same of you," replied Brassbuttons.

"The crew called me Fiddlefingers, seeing as I was always playing this fiddle," said the sailor. "I've been stuck here, all alone, for more years than I can remember."

"A fiddle player, you say? Then 'tis good fortune we found you!" boomed Brassbuttons.

No sooner had they welcomed Fiddlefingers aboard *The Jolly Jig* than he began to play. But what a shock! Instead of the tuneful harmony they had so been looking forward to hearing, he made a fearful, scratching screech.

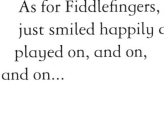

And as he played, something strange started to happen. Around them, *The Jolly Jig* began to change in a fearful way. Huge, ragged holes appeared in the sails. Timbers began to creak eerily.

"Me fingers is going transparent!" cried Jake. The ship and its pirates were turning into a *ghost* ship! Yet, strangely, Fiddlefingers didn't seem to notice.

So that gloomy day spelled doom for *The Jolly Jig*. All that could be heard as the ghost ship drifted over the oceans

were the woeful wails of her poor suffering crew, as they tried to drown out the sound of the awful fiddling.

As for Fiddlefingers, he just smiled happily and played on, and on, and on...

The Fairy Ball

Late at night when the moon is bright,
And the air is soft and still,
Pixies peep and fairies creep,
And goblins roam at will.

Elves sneak out, and slink about,
Leprechauns come leaping.
Little sprites wave magic lights,
While the world is sleeping.

Singing songs, they skip along,
Toward the forest glade.
Hung with lights, all twinkling bright,
While gentle music's played.

They appear, from far and near,
A host of fairy folk.
This happy band dance hand in hand,
Beneath the magic oak.

Where Lies the Land?

Where lies the land to which the ship would go?
Far, far ahead, is all her seamen know.
And where the land she travels from? Away,
Far, far behind, is all that they can say.
On sunny noons upon the deck's smooth face,
Linked arm in arm, how pleasant here to pace;
Or, o'er the stern reclining, watch below
The foaming wake far widening as we go.

On stormy nights when wild northwesters rave,
How proud a thing to fight with wind and wave!
The dripping sailor on the reeling mast
Exults to bear, and scorns to wish it past.
Where lies the land to which the ship would go?
Far, far ahead, is all her seamen know.
And where the land she travels from? Away,
Far, far behind, is all that they can say.

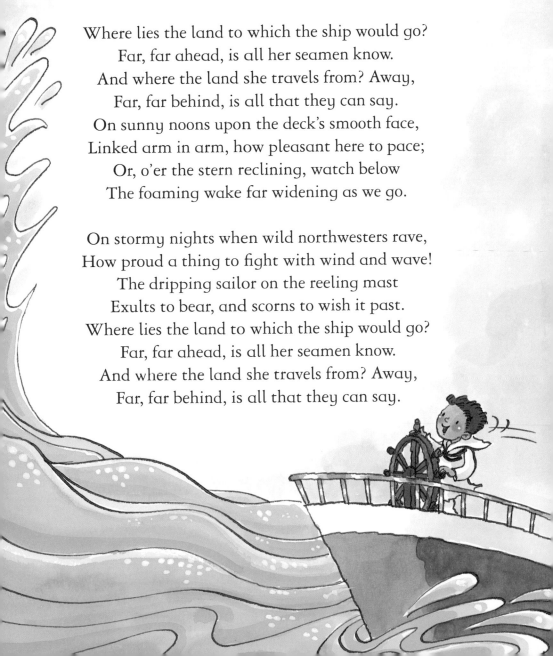

Ice Cool Duel

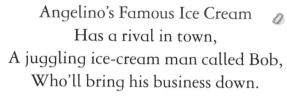

Angelino's Famous Ice Cream
Has a rival in town,
A juggling ice-cream man called Bob,
Who'll bring his business down.

Bob, who's not such a nice fellow,
Says, "Angelino, I want you out,
We'll have a juggling contest,
And the winner keeps the route."

Angelino keeps his cool, though,
Knows that he will be just fine.
What goes up a plain old cone,
Comes down a lemon and lime.

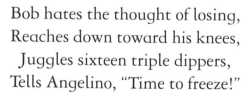

Bob hates the thought of losing,
Reaches down toward his knees,
Juggles sixteen triple dippers,
Tells Angelino, "Time to freeze!"

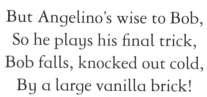

But Angelino's wise to Bob,
So he plays his final trick,
Bob falls, knocked out cold,
By a large vanilla brick!

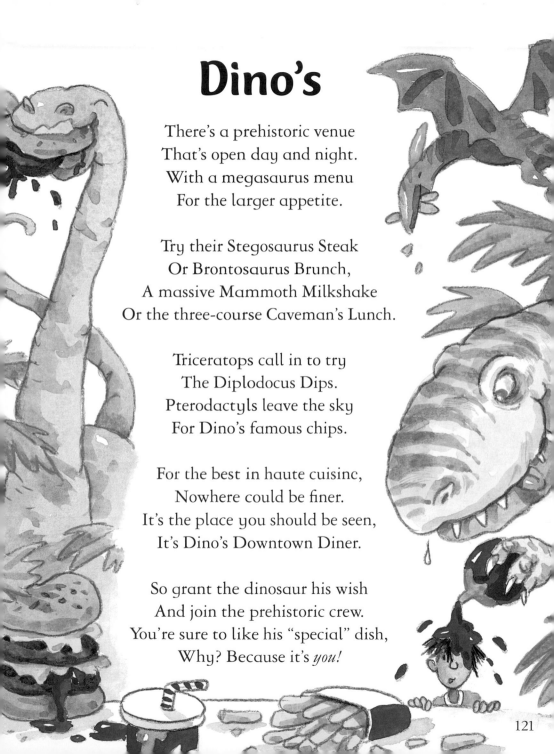

Dino's

There's a prehistoric venue
That's open day and night.
With a megasaurus menu
For the larger appetite.

Try their Stegosaurus Steak
Or Brontosaurus Brunch,
A massive Mammoth Milkshake
Or the three-course Caveman's Lunch.

Triceratops call in to try
The Diplodocus Dips.
Pterodactyls leave the sky
For Dino's famous chips.

For the best in haute cuisine,
Nowhere could be finer.
It's the place you should be seen,
It's Dino's Downtown Diner.

So grant the dinosaur his wish
And join the prehistoric crew.
You're sure to like his "special" dish,
Why? Because it's *you!*

The Greedy Crows

It was milking time on Bluebell Farm and Farmer Jones was on his way to the cowshed. Mrs. Jones, Farmer Jones's wife, came out of the farmhouse. She was wearing her dressy clothes.

"I'm off to Sunnybridge market to do some shopping, Farmer Jones," she called to him. "Is there anything you need?"

"No, thanks!" said Farmer Jones. "You look very dressy!"

"Thank you," said Mrs. Jones. "You look like a scarecrow!"

"But I always dress like this," said Farmer Jones, looking down at his patched overalls.

"That must be why you always look like a scarecrow," laughed Mrs. Jones.

Later, Farmer Jones was in the milking parlor singing along to the radio when Max the sheepdog rushed in, barking.

"What is it?" asked Farmer Jones. As he followed Max out of the barn he could hear loud squawks coming from the cornfield. Farmer Jones began to run.

"Not those greedy crows again!" he cried. And, sure enough, a flock of crows was pecking away at Farmer Jones's lovely corn.

Farmer Jones raced around the field flapping his arms. But the crows just flew out of the way for a moment, then went back to their corn feast. "Can't catch us!" they cawed.

"I've got an idea!" said Farmer Jones suddenly.

"I know just what will get rid of those greedy crows!" And he
ran off across the field and disappeared into his workshop.
Soon the air was filled with a sound of hammering and sawing.

"Uh-oh!" said Pansy the pig. "It sounds like Farmer Jones is
making something. And that usually means trouble."

Hours later, the workshop door swung open and a strange-
looking machine rattled into sight.

"Introducing the Thingymajig!" cried Farmer Jones from
behind the steering wheel.

The animals ran for cover as the
Thingymajig crashed, banged, and
walloped its way toward the
cornfield.

"Look out, you greedy
crows!" chuckled Farmer
Jones. "Here I come!"

He pulled a heavy lever and turned a huge dial. Out shot two tennis balls.

"Woof!" warned Max, as one tennis ball bounced on Pansy's bottom and landed in the water barrel. The second ball nearly hit the crows... but they just ducked.

"This isn't going to work!" thought Max.

"Take that!" Farmer Jones cried, fumbling with the lever. The Thingymajig began to rumble and rock. A spring flew into the air, spun around, and knocked Farmer Jones into the duck pond. Then the Thingymajig collapsed into a heap.

"Caw! Caw! Caw!" laughed the crows.

Farmer Jones was soaked from head to toe. "It looks like I'll never get rid of those greedy crows," he said.

Back at the farmhouse, he emptied out his rubber boots, then took off his hat and overalls. He was just hanging them on an old rake handle to dry when Mrs. Jones arrived home.

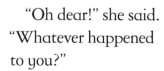

"Oh dear!" she said. "Whatever happened to you?"

"It's a long story," said Farmer Jones. "But the long and short of it is I fell into the duck pond."

"It's a good thing I bought you these, then," smiled Mrs. Jones. And she gave Farmer Jones a bag. Inside were a new hat, shirt, overalls, and rubber boots.

Farmer Jones looked at his new clothes and looked at his old clothes. Then he remembered what Mrs. Jones had said that morning. He grabbed both sets of clothes.

"I've got an idea!" he shouted.

Five minutes later, Farmer Jones came out of his workshop carrying a scarecrow wearing his old clothes.

Max and Farmer Jones carried the scarecrow down to the cornfield. The crows took one look at the scarecrow...

... and disappeared in fright!

Hector Protector

Hector Protector was dressed all in green;
Hector Protector was sent to the Queen.
The Queen did not like him,
No more did the King;
So Hector Protector
Was sent back again.

Higglety, Pigglety, Pop!

Higglety, pigglety, pop!
The dog has eaten the mop;
The pig's in a hurry,
The cat's in a flurry,
Higglety, pigglety, pop!

If Wishes Were Horses

If wishes were horses,
Beggars would ride;
If turnips were watches,
I'd wear one by my side.

Cushy Cow Bonny

Cushy cow bonny, let down thy milk,
And I will give thee a gown of silk;
A gown of silk and a silver tee,
If thou wilt let down thy milk for me.

There Was a Piper

There was a piper, he'd a cow,
And he'd no hay to give her;
He took his pipes and played a tune:
"Consider, old cow, consider!"
The cow considered very well,
For she gave the piper a penny,
That he might play the tune again,
Of "Corn rigs are bonnie."

Tom, Tom, the Piper's Son

Tom, Tom, the piper's son,
Stole a pig, and away he run.
The pig was eat, and Tom was beat,
And Tom went roaring down the street.

I Love You, Grandpa

Little Bear and Grandpa were walking by the river when Little Bear spotted a fish darting through the water.

"Quick, Grandpa!" he yelled. He rushed into the river, caught the fish, and held it up proudly for Grandpa to see.

Grandpa smiled. "My legs were once strong and speedy like yours," he said. "But now I've found an easier way to catch a meal."

"Really, Grandpa?" asked Little Bear. "What's that?"

"Well," replied Grandpa, "I'm more crafty now. I stand here at the rapids and I wait until the fish jump out of the water… straight into my mouth."

"Wow!" said Little Bear. "I love you, Grandpa. You're so clever!"

Just then, Eagle swooped down. The beat of his wings ruffled the bears' fur. They saw his sharp claws.

Little Bear ran straight up a tree. Grandpa smiled.

"I can remember when I could climb as well as you," he said. "But now I don't need to run away."

"Really, Grandpa?" asked Little Bear. "What do you do?"

"Well," replied Grandpa, "I'm bolder now." When Eagle swooped again, Grandpa barked in his deep, gruff voice. He roared, and Eagle swerved away over the mountains.

"Wow!" said Little Bear. "I love you, Grandpa. You're so brave!"

They walked on until they came across a slope where the earth was softer and deeper.

"Watch me, Grandpa!" called Little Bear. "I can dig myself a really good hollow to sleep in through the winter."

Grandpa smiled. "I can remember when I could dig as well as you," he sighed. "But now I know a better way to find a hollow."

"Really, Grandpa?" frowned Little Bear. "But where do you spend the winter?"

"Well," replied Grandpa, "I'm wiser now. All I need to do is to find a hollow tree. Follow me." And he led Little Bear to a huge tree.

In the middle of its massive trunk was a snug hollow.

"I love you, Grandpa," said Little Bear. "You know so much. Will I ever be as crafty, brave, and wise as you?"

"Of course you will!" replied Grandpa.

Soon soft flakes of snow began to fall. Inside the hollow, Little Bear snuggled up to Grandpa.

"I love you, Grandpa," he said again.

Grandpa ruffled Little Bear's messy head. "I love you too, Little Bear," Grandpa said.

Yankee Doodle

Yankee Doodle went to town,
Riding on a pony;
He stuck a feather in his hat,
And called it macaroni.
Yankee Doodle fa, so, la,
Yankee Doodle dandy,
Yankee Doodle fa, so, la,
Buttermilk and brandy.

Yankee Doodle went to town
To buy a pair of trousers,
He swore he could not see the town
For so many houses.
Yankee Doodle fa, so, la,
Yankee Doodle dandy,
Yankee Doodle fa, so, la,
Buttermilk and brandy.

Cat of Cats

I am the cat of cats. I am
The everlasting cat!
Cunning, and old, and sleek as jam,
The everlasting cat!
I hunt the vermin in the night—
The everlasting cat!
For I see best without the light—
The everlasting cat!

The Hare and the Tortoise

Once upon a time, there was a hare who was always boasting about how fast he was.

One day, much to everyone's surprise, after Hare had been boasting even more than normal, Tortoise said, "Okay, Hare. I'll race you."

"Whaaaaat?" laughed Hare. "You've got to be joking." He laughed so much that he fell to his knees and thumped the floor with his fist. "Tortoise, you're the slowest animal in the forest. I'll run circles around you!" he said.

There was a buzz of excitement in the forest the next morning.

"On your marks, get set… *Go!*" cried the starting fox.

And Hare flew off at high speed, leaving a cloud of smoke where he had just stood. The tortoise trudged behind much, much, much more slowly.

Hare decided to take a quick look behind to see where the slow tortoise was. When he saw that Tortoise was far, far away, he decided to stop for breakfast. He feasted on some juicy carrots. Then he lay on his back, fiddled with his ears, and yawned.

"This is just too easy," he said. "I think I'll have forty winks and catch up with him later." Soon he was fast asleep.

Tortoise plodded on and on. He got to where Hare was lying, fast asleep, and plodded past. He plodded on and on. Hare slept, on and on.

Suddenly Hare awoke with a jolt. He could just see Tortoise in the distance, plodding slowly and carefully toward the finish line.

"Noooooooo!" cried Hare. He leaped to his feet and charged towards the finish as fast as he could. But he was too late.

Tortoise was over the line before him. Hare had been beaten.

After that, whenever anyone heard Hare boasting about his speed they reminded him about the day Tortoise beat him.

"Slow and steady won the race," they would say, laughing.

And all Hare could do was smile because, after all, they were right.

Seal Song

You shouldn't swim till you're six weeks old,
Or your head will be sunk by your heels;
And summer gales and killer whales
Are bad for baby seals.
Are bad for baby seals, dear rat,
As bad as bad can be;
But splash and grow strong,
And you can't be wrong,
Child of the Open Sea!

Pirate Song

Fifteen men on the dead man's chest—
Yo ho ho and a bottle of rum!
Drink and the devil had done for the rest—
Yo ho ho and a bottle of rum!

Tricky Tractor

One sunny morning, Farmer Fred looked around his farmyard.

"Everything is neat and tidy," he smiled. But then he noticed the tractor. "That old tractor is past its best," he said. "It looks like the junkyard for you."

Farmer Fred jumped into the tractor and turned the key. Nothing happened. He jumped out of the tractor and untied the hood.

"Hmm, this is going to be tricky," he thought, scratching his head. "How am I going to get this old tractor to the junkyard now?"

Suddenly, Farmer Fred stood up. "Never fear, I've got an idea!"

As Farmer Fred disappeared into his workshop, the animals gathered around.

"Poor old tractor," sighed Harry Horse. "All it needs is some..."

But before Harry Horse had finished, Farmer Fred came out of the workshop.

"This," said Farmer Fred, "is my Lift-and-tow Crane. Just the thing for towing tractors."

Farmer Fred attached the Lift-and-tow Crane to the back of his pickup truck, and started cranking the back of the tractor off the ground.

"I'll tow this old tractor out of here before you can say Brussels sprouts!" he shouted, revving his engine.

Suddenly, there was a loud *Crunch!* The Lift-and-tow Crane crumpled and the tractor crashed to the ground.

"Tearaway turnips!" yelled Farmer Fred. "How am I going to move this old tractor now?"

While Farmer Fred sat thinking, Patch brought over a paintbrush. Farmer Fred smiled. "I've got a great idea—I'll spring-clean the tractor instead!"

Farmer Fred got to work right away.

First of all, he gave the tractor a good wash.

Then he oiled the hood and gave it a coat of bright red paint.

Last of all, he filled it up with gas and turned the key.

The engine coughed... and spluttered to life.

Farmer Fred and the animals stood back to admire his handiwork.

Farmer Fred smiled. "As I've always said, there's years left in my trusty tractor yet."

"Woof! Woof!" said Patch.

Mad Monsters

Squeak! Squeak!
Monster fun!
Orange tickles everyone!

Squeak! Squeak!
Clumsy Green
Has the biggest feet you've ever seen!

Squeak! Squeak!
Silly Red,
Hiding underneath the bed!

Squeak! Squeak!
Snoozy Yellow.
Fast asleep, the lazy fellow!

Squeak! Squeak!
What a noise!
Purple plays with all his toys.

Squeak! Squeak!
Pretty Pink!
She looks lovely, don't you think?

Mystery Monster

You wake with a start,
In the still of the night,
With your toes all exposed,
And your quilt pulled up tight.

You open your eyes,
You stare through the gloom,
Strange shadows loom large,
On the walls of your room.

You hear a loud creak,
As the monster draws near,
And the more that you listen,
The more that you hear.

Then you see its weird shape,
At the end of your bed,
With long skinny legs,
And a great lumpy head.

So you switch on the light,
And you whisper, "Who's there?"
But it's only your clothes,
Hanging over the chair!

Tiger Tales

Louis and Lisa Lion were just learning to pounce. One day, as they pounced through the jungle, Louis suddenly saw a flash of orange and black in some bushes.

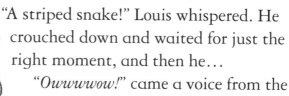

"A striped snake!" Louis whispered. He crouched down and waited for just the right moment, and then he…

"*Owwwwow!*" came a voice from the bush. "What's got my tail?"

The "snake" turned out to be attached to a striped little cub.

"Who are you?" asked Louis and Lisa.

"I'm Timmy Tiger," said the little cub. "My mom and dad and I have just moved here from The Other Side of the Jungle."

"We're Louis and Lisa Lion," said Lisa. "Would you like to see what this side of the jungle looks like?"

Timmy said he would love to.

"That's our river," said Louis proudly. "It's really muddy, and fun to swim in."

"It's very nice," said Timmy, "but it's kind of small. On The Other Side of the Jungle, there's a river that's as wide as fifty tall palm trees laid end to end, and I once swam across it!"

A little farther along, Louis and Lisa saw Howard Hippo wallowing merrily in the mud. "Hi, Howard!" they called.

"You know," said Timmy, "on The Other Side of the Jungle there's a hippo whose mouth is so big that I can sit inside it!"

"Wow!" said Lisa.

"And," Timmy continued, "my dad's twice as big as an elephant, and he can carry six gorillas on his back! And..."

Timmy stopped in his tracks. In front of him stood two tigers, smiling. They were his mom and dad.

"Mom and Dad, these are my new friends, Louis and Lisa."

"We're delighted to meet you," said Mr. and Mrs. Tiger.

"And as you can see," Mr. Tiger added, "we are very ordinary and normal tigers."

"Timmy told us some amazing things about The Other Side of the Jungle," said Louis.

Timmy looked embarrassed.

Mrs. Tiger turned to Louis and Lisa. "Timmy didn't have any friends to play with on The Other Side of the Jungle, so he spent all his time imagining amazing adventures."

"But now that he has friends like you two to play with," said Mr. Tiger, "perhaps he'll have some real adventures, like the ones in his stories!"

Jack Be Nimble

Jack be nimble,
And Jack be quick:
And Jack jump over
The candlestick.

The Man in the Wilderness

I met a man in the wilderness with a funny notion,
He asked me, "How many strawberries grow in the ocean?"
I answered him as I thought good,
As many red herrings as grow in the wood.

Fire on the Mountain

Rats in the garden—catch 'em Towser!
Cows in the cornfield—run boys run!
Cat's in the cream pot—stop her now, sir!
Fire on the mountain—run boys run!

If All the World Was Apple Pie

If all the world was apple pie,
And all the ocean ink,
And all the trees were bread and cheese,
What should we have for drink?

This Little Piggy

This little piggy went to market,
This little piggy stayed at home,
This little piggy had roast beef,
This little piggy had none,
And this little piggy cried,
Wee-wee-wee-wee-wee
All the way home.

Bob Robin

Little Bob Robin,
Where do you live?
Up in yonder wood, sir,
On a hazel twig.

Perfect Turns

"How's your swimming training going?" Sophia asked her brother, as she scooped up a spoonful of breakfast cereal.

Daniel shrugged. "I'm not getting any faster and the school swimming meet is only three weeks away." He picked up his school bag.

"Adam Blade's pretty good," Sophia observed. "You'll have to work hard to beat him."

"I know," Daniel replied as he left for the pool. "He trains every morning, like me."

Sophia kept on eating her breakfast. Daniel had set his heart on winning the 200-meter freestyle race. He wanted the prize—four free tickets to see the new *Pirates* film. But so did Adam Blade.

Daniel shivered as he stood with his toes over the edge of the pool. Adam was already speeding through the water.

Daniel took a deep breath and dived in. He swam slowly at first. As his muscles grew warm he began to swim faster. He passed Adam a few times, but, just as often, Adam passed him.

"Daniel!" a muffled voice shouted.

Daniel finished his lap and looked up. It was Sophia. "What are you doing here?" he asked.

Sophia dangled her feet in the water. "I decided to watch you training," she replied.

Daniel sighed. "I think I'm losing time in my turns," he said.

Sophia looked over at Adam. She watched as he came to the end of a lap, flipped over, and pushed away from the wall. "Wow," she said. "Did you see that?"

Daniel watched Adam swim to the other side of the pool. "See what?" he asked.

"Adam's turns are perfect," Sophia told him. "He hardly slows down. Watch."

Adam performed another rapid turn and then headed toward them.

Daniel was quiet as he studied Adam's swimming stroke. "You know, if he kept his legs straighter and pointed his toes more, he would swim faster."

Sophia nodded. "And if you improved your turns, you'd make better time, too."

Adam reached the end of the pool.

Daniel cupped his hands around his mouth.

"Adam!" he yelled.

Adam stopped. He shook water from his hair and looked at the twins.

"I have an idea," Daniel told him. "I can help you improve your stroke if you help me with my turns."

Adam looked uncertain at first. Then he pulled himself out of the pool and sat on the side. "Sounds good to me," he grinned.

A few days later, it was the day of the swimming meet.

"The 200-meter freestyle," Miss Travers announced. "Swimmers, take your positions."

Daniel took his place at the side of the pool. Adam did the same.

The whistle blew and Daniel hit the water. He sped to the other side of the pool, remembering what Adam had taught him: he had to get closer to the wall before he turned, so he could get a stronger push with his legs.

Getting as close to the wall as he could, Daniel flipped over and pushed off again. Adam was right beside him in the next lane. Adam's stroke had sped up, thanks to Daniel's advice.

Daniel pushed himself harder. But he couldn't shake off Adam. There he was—level with Daniel, length after length.

At last, Daniel's hand slapped against the tiles. The race was over. He stood up. Beside him, Adam did the same.

Who had won?

Miss Travers looked at her stopwatch and walked slowly toward the boys, a huge smile on her face. "You have both broken your own records!" she told them. "And you both hold the new one!"

"Both of us?" asked Adam.

"It was a tie?" asked Daniel.

"That's right," said Miss Travers. "Congratulations! You share the prize. Two movie tickets each. Nice work, boys!"

Welcome to the Haunted House!

Step in through the rusty gates—
Be quiet as a mouse.
We're going to sneak, and take
A peek, inside the Haunted House!

Upstairs in the dusty bedrooms
Skeletons are getting dressed.
Vampires brush their hair and teeth.
All the spooks must look their best!

An empty suit of shiny armor
Is clanking loudly down the hall,
To a party in the ballroom—
It's the Spooks' Secret Ball!

So while the party's in full swing,
Be quiet as a mouse.
Tiptoe out while you still can—
Escape the Haunted House!

Five Little Monkeys

Five little monkeys walked along the shore;
One went a-sailing,
Then there were four.
Four little monkeys climbed up a tree;
One of them tumbled down,
Then there were three.
Three little monkeys found a pot of glue;
One got stuck in it,
Then there were two.
Two little monkeys found a currant bun;
One ran away with it,
Then there was one.
One little monkey cried all afternoon,
So they put him in an airplane
And sent him to the moon.

Car Wash Charlie

One sunny Saturday, Ryan and his dad were washing the car.

"Woof!" barked Charlie the dog.

"I think Charlie wants to help, too," said Ryan.

Dad looked at Charlie's muddy paws. "I'm not sure muddy dogs are very good at washing cars," he said. "But I guess he can watch."

The first thing Ryan and his dad did was to splash water all over the car to get rid of the worst dirt. Charlie jumped around excitedly, chasing a blue butterfly.

Then Dad put some car soap in a bucket. "We need to go into the kitchen and fill this with water," he said.

When they came back, Dad looked at the car with a puzzled expression on his face.

"I was sure I'd rinsed that bit," he said, looking at a muddy smear on the side of the car and waving away the butterfly, which had settled on the side mirror.

Ryan and Dad got to work with their sponges, washing and rinsing the first side of the car. The soap made *loads* of bubbles! Charlie tried to eat some, but he didn't like the taste.

"Now the second side," said Dad. "But let's have a drink first."

In the kitchen, Dad had a cup of coffee and Ryan had a glass of orange juice. Then they filled up their buckets and went back out to the car.

"Look, Ryan," said Dad. "I think you missed a bit."

Sure enough, above the wheel was a muddy bit.

"Sorry, Dad," said Ryan. But it was strange—he was sure he could remember washing that bit!

The two of them washed the other side of the car. The butterfly fluttered around Ryan's head, while Charlie

nosed around in the puddles of water on the floor.

"Right!" said Dad, when they had finished. "Now we need to go and get some old towels from the garage to dry it with."

Ryan and Dad went to the garage. "Can you stand on the chair and get the towels on that top shelf?" asked Dad.

Ryan stood on the chair and stretched for the towels. Then, through the window he saw Charlie—jumping onto the hood of the freshly washed car in hot pursuit of the butterfly!

"Look, Dad!" cried Ryan.

"*Charlie*!" shouted Dad, running out of the garage.

Charlie jumped off the hood. He looked very guilty.

Dad started to laugh. "I think we know now where those muddy smears came from," he said. "Time for you to go inside, Charlie. And after we've finished washing the car, our next job's going to be to wash *you*!"

Creepy Castle

In a castle, dark and dusty,
Stood an armor suit all rusty.
Haunted from breastplate to visor,
Visitors were none the wiser.

Then, one day, the suit went walking,
Past some tourists who were talking.
How they stared with big, round eyes.
Some let out astonished cries!

"This way! Run!" the tour guide said,
And everybody soon had fled.
The empty suit marched down the hall,
And shut the door on one and all!

Soon the news spread far and wide
And lines of tourists formed outside.
A great big crowd had come to see,
The clanking ghost that wandered free.

The empty suit was most perplexed
(And not to say a little vexed).
He'd meant to scare them all away—
And so he left that very day!

Where Animals Rule

In the land where the animals rule,
The children don't go to school.
They live on farms, and flap their arms,
Just like the chickens used to do.

Jaguars and speeding cheetahs,
Are stopped when they go too fast
By policing cats in pointed hats,
Who yowl when they whiz past.

If you go for a round-the-world sail,
You travel on the back of a whale.
Hold on for dear life when he starts to dive,
And look out for that over-sized tail.

It's fun where the animals rule,
No one tells you what you ought to do.
Their idea of fun is to sleep in the sun,
It's just the place for a person like you.

Monsters Everywhere

In the jungles and the valleys,
In the closet by the stairs,
In the bedroom, in the kitchen,
You'll find monsters everywhere!

Find a lake, a pond, a puddle,
Anywhere that fishes swim,
There's just one thing you can be sure of,
Down below there's something grim.

Steal a look inside a pyramid,
Just be careful when you do,
If you wake a sleeping mummy
He'll come clomping after you!

Trek into the craggy mountains
Where the snow lies all year long,
If you listen to the silence
You can hear the yeti's song.

Gaze into the starry twilight,
You might glimpse a UFO,
Could it be from outer space?
You will never really know.

Hunting Song of the Seeone Pack

As the dawn was breaking the Sambhur belled
Once, twice, and again!
And a doe leaped up, and a doe leaped up,
From the pond in the wood where the wild deer sup.
This I, scouting alone, beheld,
Once, twice, and again!

As the dawn was breaking the Sambhur belled
Once, twice, and again!
And a wolf stole back, and a wolf stole back,
To carry the word to the waiting pack,
And we sought and we found and we bayed on his track,
Once, twice, and again!

As the dawn was breaking the Sambhur belled
Once, twice, and again!
Feet in the jungle that leave no mark!
Eyes that can see in the dark—the dark!
Tongue—give tongue to it! Hark! Oh hark!
Once, twice, and again!

The Powerful Spell

The sky went black and the villagers ran for their lives.
"Help! Help!" they cried, as they dashed for the safety of
the castle. "The dragon is back!"

Hovering above the thick stone castle walls, its giant
red, scaly wings outstretched, was a huge and terrible
dragon.

"Curses!" snarled the dragon, blasting the castle
with fire. "Just missed a tasty bite to eat."

The village had been a target for the dragon
almost every day since it had taken up residence in
the nearby mountains. Fortunately, help was on
hand—from a very unlikely source.

Alberta the absent-minded witch happened to
zoom over the mountains on her broomstick, just
as the dragon was returning to its nest. Alberta,
who always traveled too fast and who never
looked where she was going, sailed right into the
dragon's open mouth.

Now, to find yourself stuck in the
foul-smelling mouth of a dragon

would be enough to send even the nicest witch off the deep end. "Newts and toads!" she snapped, thinking the dragon had had the cheek to try to eat her. "You've bitten off a bit more than you can chew this time!"

Raising her magic wand, she cast a brilliant spell: *"A fearsome dragon you will not be. I'll wave this wand, just wait and see!"*

Then she conjured herself back to the comfort of her own home for a cup of slime tea.

Blissfully ignorant of the fact that a powerful spell had been cast upon it, the dragon returned to its nest.

"Dragon ahoy!" shouted the lookout the next day, as the dragon swooped down on the village once more. But the dreaded fiery jets of dragon breath never came, for when the enchanted dragon drew a deep breath and blew out with all its might, millions of sweet-smelling flower petals fluttered downward from its gaping jaws.

Inside the castle, everyone started to laugh.

The dragon knew it was making a ridiculous spectacle of itself. No dragon worth its salt would blast a castle with flower petals! It flew away and never came back.

"Good riddance to you," the king called after the dragon.

Then everyone enjoyed a wonderful celebratory feast, before they lived happily ever after.

I'm a Big Brother!

Luke was very excited. Grandma and Grandpa had been looking after him, but now Mommy and Daddy were home.

And they had a wonderful surprise—a new baby!

"The baby is so tiny!" said Luke.

"You were this tiny once," said Daddy. "But now you're big—you're Baby's big brother!"

"Can I play with Baby?" Luke asked.

"Soon," said Mommy. "But right now Baby needs to sleep." She put the baby in a crib.

"I'll wait until the baby wakes up," Luke thought. "Then maybe we'll be able to play." But the baby woke up, and was still too tiny to play with Luke!

And the baby was still too tiny to play the next day, and the day after, and the day after that!

"You need to wait just a bit longer," Mommy said.

All Baby seemed to do was sleep or cry or eat, or need a clean diaper.

"I wish Baby would hurry up and grow!" Luke said every day.

One morning, when Luke looked into Baby's crib, Baby was smiling—and sitting up!

Luke was so excited that he called Mommy and Daddy.

"Baby's getting bigger," they told Luke.

"Big enough to play with me?" asked Luke, holding up his toy airplane.

"Not big enough to play airplanes with you," Daddy explained. "You'll have to wait a bit longer for that."

Later, Luke watched as Daddy fed the baby. "Is Baby ever going to be big enough to play with me?" Luke asked.

"Yes," said Daddy. "You were once as little as Baby, but you got big enough to play—and Baby will, too!" And Baby did start to grow. Baby grew bigger... and bigger!

Luke learned how to help dress Baby and how to help feed Baby. Baby was a very messy eater!

"Baby is lucky to have a helpful big brother like you," said Daddy.

One afternoon, Mommy said to Luke, "Let's take Baby to the park."

"Will Baby be able to play in the sandbox with me? Or come on the swings?" Luke asked.

"Not just yet," said Mommy. "But Baby would love to watch you! A big brother can show Baby all sorts of things."

At the park, Luke rushed to the sandbox. "I'll show Baby how to make a sandcastle!" he said.

Baby watched happily while Luke built a wonderful sandcastle.

"It's even more fun when Baby watches," Luke said.

"I think Baby is having fun, too!" said Mommy.

That night, Luke said he would like to help Mommy give Baby a bath.

While Mommy washed Baby, Luke sailed a boat through the bubbles and made little splashes in the water.

Baby laughed and kicked and splashed, too. It was a lot of fun—almost like playing with Baby!

A few days later, Luke was playing with his train in the living room. Suddenly, Baby crawled over and grabbed the engine!

"Mommy! Daddy!" cried Luke. "Baby is taking my train! Make Baby stop!"

"I think Baby is trying to tell you something," Mommy said.

"What?" Luke asked.

"I think," said Mommy, "that Baby is saying... 'I'm ready to play with you now!'"

"Hooray!" cried Luke. He ran to the toy box and picked up a soft, squishy ball.

"Catch!" said Luke, as he rolled the ball to Baby. Baby laughed and tried to catch the ball. Luke rolled the ball to Baby again, and this time Baby grabbed it.

Baby laughed, and Luke laughed, too.

He rolled the ball to Baby again and again. "I think," Luke said to Mommy and Daddy, "that being a big brother is going to be *lots* of fun from now on!"

And it was!

To Market, to Market

To market, to market, to buy a fat pig,
Home again, home again, dancing a jig;
Ride to the market to buy a fat hog,
Home again, home again, jiggety-jog.

To Market, to Market

To market, to market, to buy a plum bun;
Home again, home again, market is done.

Two Little Men

Two little men in a flying saucer
Flew around the world one day.
They looked left and right,
And they didn't like the sight,
So then they flew away!

Higgledy Piggledy

Higgledy piggledy,
Here we lie,
Picked and plucked,
And put in a pie!

Jack, Jack, the Bread's a-Burning

Jack, Jack, the bread's a-burning,
All to a cinder;
If you don't come and fetch it out
We'll throw it through the window.

My Rabbit

I love my rabbit,
Who's soft and furry,
And wiggles his nose
All the time—it's his habit.

Howls and Owls

"Owwww!" A horrible howl rang out through the darkness. Beneath the moon, Hairy the Horrible Hound sat staring at his paws. He had been howling away all evening. He wanted someone to talk to, someone to play with. But because he was a ghost hound no one would come near.

The moon shone between the clouds and lit up the ruined manor house on top of the hill. The people who once lived there had fled years ago. Now it was just the haunt of Shiver, an old ghost.

Shiver was resting. At the first sound of Hairy's howls, he groaned. "Hairy's dreadful noise goes right through my skull!" he cried. "Something must be done!"

"Who's Hairy?" a voice above Shiver asked. An owl flitted through a hole in the roof.

"Hairy is the ghost hound who howls horribly outside in the lane," said Shiver. "I wish he would stop."

"He might, if you ask him nicely," blinked the owl.

"M-me? Face Hairy the Horrible Hound?" breathed Shiver.

"Well, someone should!" said the

owl. "I only flew in yesterday and I must say, I'm tired of that howling already! I suppose I'll have to do it myself."

Soon the owl was back. But this time he wasn't alone! There was a padding of paws on the front steps, then the door swung open on its creaky hinges.

"Yikes! Time I disappeared!" trembled Shiver. But it was too late! In swept the owl, followed by the ghostly hound.

"Hairy told me he only howls because he's lonely," said the owl. "He chases anything that moves, too, in the hope of finding a friend! If you want my advice, you should let him come and live here. What better than a ghostly guard dog?"

"I promise I'd never howl again," pleaded Hairy, hopefully.

"You can lie beside my old bed, Hairy," smiled Shiver, who wasn't the least bit nervous now.

And so Hairy the Horrible Hound found a home at last.

But if Shiver had hoped for some peace and quiet, he was to be sadly disappointed. For if Hairy wasn't playfully pulling the sheets off Shiver, he was leaping onto his lap for company.

Slowly, though, Shiver grew to like things being more lively. Which was just as well, or Hairy might have had to start howling again!

When Monsters Go to Costume Parties

What is it like for a monster
When they're asked to a costume do?
Do they dress up in a human costume
And go as a person like you?

Do they put on their best outfits
And think of polite things to say?
Nibble no more than a modest amount
And dance in a fashionable way?

Monsters aren't good at pretending.
They gulp down their food in one go.
When they take to the floor for a tango,
They jerk and they stamp to and fro.

No, monsters will always be monstrous.
It's a fact that you just cannot hide.
You might make a monster look human,
But you can't change the monster inside.

The Timid Troll

Timothy the Timid Troll
Though horrible and hairy,
Had a meek, mild-mannered streak
That simply wasn't scary.

He said to Mom, all misty eyed,
"I'd like to learn to sing."
His father said, "Don't be absurd,
Who's heard of such a thing?"

And though Tim tried with all his might
The highest notes to reach,
All that he could manage was
A shrill and evil screech.

A sound that froze the very soul
And made the windows crack.
"That's our boy," said Mom to Dad
And slapped him on the back.

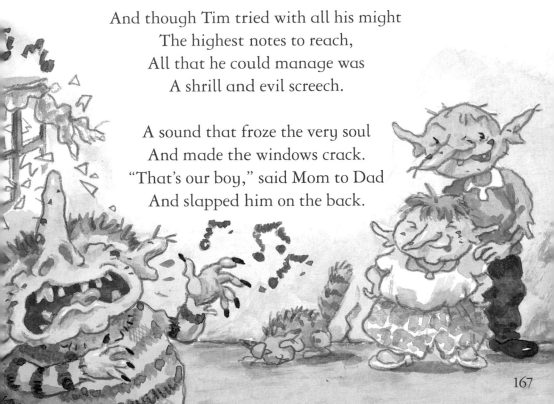

Space School Star

As soon as he woke up, Ethan knew something was wrong. He looked at his clock—it was nine o'clock! Today was the day of his junior astronaut test, and he should have been at school fifteen minutes ago.

He stumbled out of bed and bumped into Dad on the way to the bathroom.

Dad made a face. "Mom left early this morning, and my alarm clock didn't go off," he complained.

"I'm late for my test!" said Ethan.

"And I'm late for work!" replied Dad. "You'll have to get yourself to school today."

Ethan got his hover boots. He could fly really fast in them. But then he remembered, they needed new batteries…

Ethan wasn't usually allowed to use the teleporting machine, but he decided this was an emergency. He pressed the buttons to key

in his destination. If he made a mistake, he could end up in another galaxy.

Taking a deep breath, he stepped in. Ethan shut his eyes and pressed *Go*.

Seconds later, he was in the exam hall. He had done it!

"Sit down, Ethan," said his teacher, Mr. Satellite. "The test is about to begin. Good luck!"

When Ethan got home, Mom looked furious. "I found your helmet in the teleporting machine," she said. "What have you been up to, Ethan? That is a very dangerous machine."

Then the satellite phone rang. Still frowning at Ethan, Mom answered it.

When she ended the call, Mom went over to Ethan. To Ethan's surprise, she gave him a hug.

"That was your teacher," she said. "You got 100 percent on your test today!"

Ethan couldn't believe his ears. "Wow!" he said.

"So I'd better let you off about the teleporting machine," Mom said with a smile. She gave Ethan his space helmet. "You'll be a great astronaut one day, Ethan, but it seems you're a pretty good one already!"

Super Snakes

One day, Seymour Snake's cousin, Sadie, came to stay.

"Sadie!" cried Seymour. "It's so good to see you! Come and meet my friends! You can play games with us, and…"

"Oh, I don't play games anymore," Sadie interrupted. "I've been going to Madame Sylvia's Snake School. Madame Sylvia always says, "'A well-behaved snake may slither and glide and wriggle and slide, but we *don't* swing or sway, or climb or play!'"

"Well, will you come and meet my friends?" Seymour asked.

"Oh, yesss," hissed Sadie. "It would be rude not to!"

"Hey, Seymour!" shouted Maxine Monkey. "Come and play Coconut Catch with Mickey and me!"

"You can come and play, too," Seymour said to Sadie.

"No, thank you," said Sadie. "I'll just watch."

Seymour spent hours hanging and swinging and climbing. Each time, Seymour invited Sadie to join him. But Sadie always said, "I shouldn't swing or sway, or climb or play."

Suddenly, Seymour had an idea.

The next day, Sadie was gliding through the jungle when she found Ellen and Emma Elephant, staring up into a tree.

"What's going on?" Sadie asked.

"We were playing Fling the Melon," said Ellen, "and the melon got stuck in that tree. We can't reach it!"

"Oh, dear," said Sadie. "I'm sure Seymour will be happy to climb up and get it for you."

But Seymour had disappeared!

"Can't you help us, Sadie?" Emma asked. "We know about Madame Sylvia's rules. But surely Madame Sylvia must have taught you that it's important to help others."

"Yes, she did," said Sadie. So up she went, winding her way up the trunk and into the branches. She found the melon and gave it a shove. It fell down into Ellen's waiting trunk.

"Thanks, Sadie!" said Emma. "Are you coming down now?"

"Er, not just yet," said Sadie. "I just want to try something first." With a quick wriggle, Sadie coiled herself round the branch and hung upside down above the elephants.

"This is *sssstupendous!*" Sadie hissed. She swung herself over to another tree. "*Wheee!*" she cried.

"I knew you'd like swinging and climbing if you gave it a try," called Seymour, coming out from where he'd been hiding.

"Come up here, Seymour!" Sadie called.

"But what will you tell Madame Sylvia?" asked Seymour.

"I'll just tell her," said Sadie, "that we *must* climb and play, and swing and sway—*all day!*"

Tumbling

In jumping and tumbling we spend the whole day,
Till night by arriving has finished our play.
What then? One and all, there's no more to be said,
As we tumbled all day, so we tumble to bed.

Lie a-Bed

Lie a-bed,
Sleepy head,
Shut up eyes, bo-peep;
'Til daybreak
Never wake—
Baby, sleep.

There Was a Crooked Man

There was a crooked man, and he went a crooked mile,
He found a crooked sixpence against a crooked stile;
He bought a crooked cat, which caught a crooked mouse,
And they all lived together in a little crooked house.

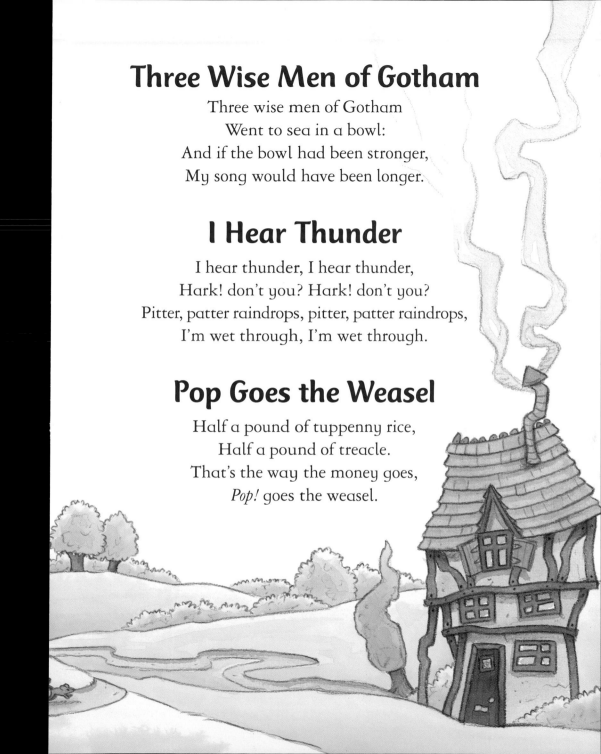

Three Wise Men of Gotham

Three wise men of Gotham
Went to sea in a bowl:
And if the bowl had been stronger,
My song would have been longer.

I Hear Thunder

I hear thunder, I hear thunder,
Hark! don't you? Hark! don't you?
Pitter, patter raindrops, pitter, patter raindrops,
I'm wet through, I'm wet through.

Pop Goes the Weasel

Half a pound of tuppenny rice,
Half a pound of treacle.
That's the way the money goes,
Pop! goes the weasel.

Storm Rescue

One windy day there was a big black cloud over the farm. There was a flash of lightning and a loud rumble of thunder.

"Come on, Patch," cried Farmer Fred. "We'll get the animals into the barn."

"Neigh!" said Harry Horse, trying to help. He plodded after Farmer Fred.

"Oh, dear," sighed Harry Horse. "I'm too slow for herding cows and sheep. Perhaps I can help the ducks and hens."

Harry Horse stamped his hoof to nudge the hens toward the barn. But his stamping hooves frightened the hens.

"I'm too big," sighed Harry. "I'm just a useless old horse."

Soon, the animals were safe in the barn. Harry Horse noticed that Polly Pig and her piglets were missing. He neighed and stamped his hoof.

Farmer Fred looked around. "Whizzing hurricanes!" he cried. "Polly and her piglets are missing."

Farmer Fred and the animals raced to Hog Hollow. The storm had blown a tree across the entrance of Polly Pig's pigpen.

"Polly and her piglets are trapped!" said Farmer Fred. "We'll have to pull that tree out of the way. The tractor won't fit through the gate. But never fear, I've got an idea!"

Farmer Fred disappeared into his workshop.

Later, he appeared, grinning. "This," he said, "is the new Mobile Handsaw. It will cut through the tree in no time!"

Farmer Fred wheeled the Mobile Handsaw to the pigpen. He flipped a switch and it roared into life. It began to rattle and shake. Then, with a loud *ping* the elastic broke.

"Let's try to lift the tree out of the way," said Farmer Fred.

Farmer Fred and the animals pushed and pulled. But it was no good—the tree wouldn't budge.

"Woof! Woof!" barked Patch, pulling at Harry's old harness.

"Hold on, I've had an idea!" cried Fred. "I know who can help me drag that tree out of the way."

Farmer Fred quickly harnessed Harry Horse. He attached some rope to the harness, and tied the rope around the tree.

"Heave!" cried Farmer Fred. Harry dug in his hooves and heaved. The tree began to slide away from the sty.

At last, Polly and her piglets were free.

"What a useful horse!" cried all the animals.

Harry Horse neighed happily. He was a useful horse, after all!

Hark the Robbers

Hark at the robbers going through,
Through, through, through; through, through, through;
Hark at the robbers going through, my fair lady.

What have the robbers done to you,
You, you, you; you, you, you?
What have the robbers done to you, my fair lady?

Stole my gold watch and chain,
Chain, chain, chain; chain, chain, chain;
Stole my gold watch and chain, my fair lady.

How many pounds will set us free,
Free, free, free; free, free, free?
How many pounds will set us free, my fair lady?

A hundred pounds will set you free,
Free, free, free; free, free, free;
A hundred pounds will set you free, my fair lady.

My Father He Died

My father he died, but I can't tell you how,
He left me six horses to drive in my plow:
With my wing wang waddle oh,
Jack sing saddle oh,
Blowsey boys bubble oh,
Under the broom.

I sold my six horses and I bought me a cow,
I'd fain have made a fortune,
But did not know how:
With my wing wang waddle oh,
Jack sing saddle oh,
Blowsey boys bubble oh,
Under the broom.

I sold my cow, and I bought me a calf;
I'd fain have made a fortune,
But lost the best half:
With my wing wang waddle oh,
Jack sing saddle oh,
Blowsey boys bubble oh,
Under the broom.

Just Perfect

Oakey looked out of the window. The lane wound over the hill and far away.

Oakey found Mom and said, "I want to go off and explore."

"You can go as far as the curve in the lane, across the big field, and then back again," Mom said.

Mom packed a carrot, an apple, and a sandwich in Oakey's bag. "In case you get hungry," she smiled.

Down the lane, Oakey heard Horse grumbling, "I'm so hungry! The farmer hasn't fed me today."

"You can have this," said Oakey, holding out his carrot.

Horse crunched the carrot noisily. "Perfect!" he grinned. "Would you like a ride?"

"I'm too busy today!" said Oakey. Halfway across the field, Oakey heard Pig groaning, "Where's the farmer? I'm really hungry!"

"Would you like this?" asked Oakey, holding out his apple.

Pig gobbled the apple greedily. "Perfect!" he grinned. "Would you like to see my trick?"

"I don't have time!" explained Oakey. "I've got the whole world to explore." And he headed towards the pond.

As he got nearer, he could hear Duck complaining. "I'm so

hungry," she quacked loudly. "I think the farmer's forgotten my bread."

"You can have mine," said Oakey, holding out his sandwich.

Duck swallowed it swiftly. "Perfect!" she grinned. "Would you like a guide on your journey?"

"I know where I'm going," answered Oakey. "I've got the whole world to explore."

And he wandered on. Oakey didn't notice the grass getting higher and higher. Suddenly, he couldn't see where he was going.

"I can see the way," quacked Duck, from above Oakey's head. "Should I lead you home?"

"Perfect!" Oakey replied. But the way home seemed very long.

"I'll never get back," sobbed Oakey.

"Cheer up!" said Pig, poking his head through the grass. He turned a cartwheel and fell flat on his nose.

"I feel much better now!" Oakey laughed.

But before long, Oakey grew tired. "I can't walk any farther," he said.

"Then how about riding on me?" neighed Horse.

"Just perfect!" smiled Oakey.

Off they went. Duck flew ahead. Pig cartwheeled along.

And Horse carried Oakey all the way home.

Where Oakey's mom was waiting... with a big hug!

Surprise Sports Star

"Oh, no! We've got Jasmine," Jason whispered to Daniel and Sophia. "She's hopeless." The class was about to play basketball.

Sophia frowned. "Give Jasmine a chance," she said.

Staring at her shoes, Jasmine walked over to her team.

Miss Travers held up the basketball. "Ready?" she called. Then she blew her whistle.

During the game, Sophia saw Jasmine shy away whenever the ball came near.

But then, near the end of the game, Daniel yelled, "Jasmine! You're closest to the net!" He threw the ball towards her.

"Catch it!" yelled Jason.

Jasmine ran forward, holding out her arms.

Sophia held her breath.

The ball slipped through Jasmine's hands and bounced off the ground.

Sammy on the other team grabbed it and headed off to the other end of the court. He steered the ball up into the air and it dropped neatly into the net.

"Score!" his team shouted.

Miss Travers blew her

whistle. The game was over.

Sophia watched Jasmine trudge from the sports hall. She hurried to catch up with her. "Cheer up, Jasmine," she said. "It's supposed to be fun."

"I know," Jasmine replied quietly. "But I'm hopeless." She shrugged and walked away.

"Did you hear about the charity fun run?" Daniel asked Sophia as they walked home. "You collect sponsors and run laps around the school track."

Just then, Jasmine sprinted around the corner with her older brother. Both of them carried bags full of newspapers.

Sophia stopped, her eyes wide. "Look!" she said. "See how fast Jasmine's running!"

"Maybe she should enter the fun run," said Daniel.

Sophia nodded and began running after Jasmine. "Hey! Jasmine!" she called.

Jasmine stopped, allowing Sophia and Daniel to catch up.

"You're so fast!" Sophia panted.

Jasmine shrugged. "We run to get the paper round finished quickly," she said.

"Well, we think you should enter the fun run," Daniel said.

Now Jasmine looked surprised. "But I'm terrible at sports," she protested.

"You're not terrible at running, and that's a sport," Sophia pointed out.

Daniel patted Jasmine's paper bag. "Think about it," he said. "You're training every day, when you help your brother."

Jasmine shuffled her feet and looked down. "I'll think about it," she said.

On the morning of the fun run, Sophia and Daniel lined up with the other runners.

Daniel nudged Sophia. "Jasmine's here," he said, pointing to the other side of the crowd.

Sophia smiled. "Great!" she said."I really hoped she would be."

"Ready, runners?" Miss Travers called. "You have one hour."

The starting whistle blew!

Sophia and Daniel began to run. A few seconds later, Jasmine sailed past.

After thirty minutes, at least half of the runners had dropped out. By fifty minutes, only a few were left running. And Jasmine was still out in front.

Miss Travers blew her whistle. "That's one hour!" she announced.

Jasmine came and sank onto the grass next to Sophia and Daniel. "You were right!" she beamed. "Running is a sport I can do well."

"Runners, gather around, please!" called Miss Travers. "You have all run like champions, but the highest number of laps was run by... Jasmine!"

Everyone cheered and clapped. Miss Travers looked very pleased.

Jasmine looked pleased and embarrassed.

"Well done!" whispered Sophia.

"And now that Jasmine has shown us what she can do, I hope she will join our cross-country running team," Miss Travers added.

Jasmine smiled with happiness. "Yes, please!" she said.

I Saw a Slippery, Slithery Snake

I saw a slippery, slithery snake
Slide through the grasses, making them shake.
He looked at me with his beady eye.
"Go away from my pretty green garden," said I.
"Sssss," said the slippery, slithery snake,
As he slid through the grasses, making them shake.

Foxy's Hole

Put your finger in
Foxy's hole.
Foxy's not at home.
Foxy's out
At the back door
A-picking at a bone.

Round About There

Round about there,
Sat a little bear,
He went to get some honey,
Right up there!

Clap, Clap Hands

Clap, clap hands, one, two, three,
Put your hands upon your knees,
Lift them up high to touch the sky,
Clap, clap hands and away they fly.

Head and Shoulders, Knees and Toes

Head and shoulders, knees and toes, knees and toes,
Head and shoulders, knees and toes, knees and toes,
And eyes, and ears, and mouth, and nose.
Head and shoulders, knees and toes, knees and toes.

Leg Over Leg

Leg over leg,
As the dog went to Dover;
When he came to a stile,
Jump he went over.

Cooking Up a Storm

I've got my biggest cauldron
Heating up upon the fire,
And I've gathered the ingredients
This fine spell will require!

A handful of cat's whiskers,
The tails from three young pups,
A big ladle full of eyeballs,
And froggy slime—two cups!

Bangs and crashes shake the windows,
It's raining cats and dogs,
Outside the storm is stirring up
A nasty shower of frogs!

For, although it may be August,
So sunny, bright, and warm,
You'd better run for cover—
I've cooked up the perfect storm!

When Dreams Come True

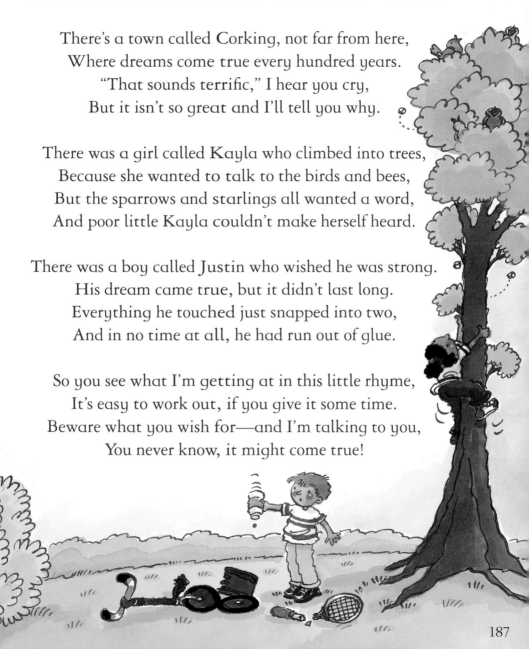

There's a town called Corking, not far from here,
Where dreams come true every hundred years.
"That sounds terrific," I hear you cry,
But it isn't so great and I'll tell you why.

There was a girl called Kayla who climbed into trees,
Because she wanted to talk to the birds and bees,
But the sparrows and starlings all wanted a word,
And poor little Kayla couldn't make herself heard.

There was a boy called Justin who wished he was strong.
His dream came true, but it didn't last long.
Everything he touched just snapped into two,
And in no time at all, he had run out of glue.

So you see what I'm getting at in this little rhyme,
It's easy to work out, if you give it some time.
Beware what you wish for—and I'm talking to you,
You never know, it might come true!

The Three Little Pigs

Once upon a time there were three little pigs. One day the three little pigs set off to find new homes.

Soon the three little pigs saw a pile of straw.

"I'll build my house of straw," said the first little pig.

The two little pigs walked on. They saw a big pile of sticks underneath an oak tree.

"I'll build my house of sticks," said the second pig.

The third little pig walked on. He saw a pile of bricks.

"I'll build a strong house of bricks," said the third little pig.

It took the third little pig a long time to build his house. His brothers laughed at him for working so hard. But the house of bricks was very strong.

The very next day, a big bad wolf called at the house of straw.

"Little pig, little pig, let me come in," said the wolf.

"Not by the hair of my chinny chin chin!" said the first little pig. So the wolf huffed and he puffed and he blew the house down.

The little pig ran away

and hid with his brother in the house of sticks.

The next day, the big bad wolf called at the house of sticks.

"Little pig, little pig, let me come in," he said.

"Not by the hair of my chinny chin chin!" said the second little pig. So the wolf huffed and he puffed and he blew the house down.

The two little pigs ran away and hid with their brother in the house of bricks.

The next day, the big bad wolf called at the house of bricks.

"Little pig, little pig, let me come in," said the wolf.

"Not by the hair of my chinny chin chin!" said the third little pig. So the wolf huffed and he puffed. But he couldn't blow the house down.

The big bad wolf was very cross. "I'm coming down the chimney to eat you!" he cried.

The third little pig made a fire under the chimney. Then he put a pot of water on the fire.

The big bad wolf climbed down the chimney and *Splash!* He fell into the pot of hot water.

"Help! Help!" cried the wolf. He jumped out of the pot and ran out of the house.

And he was never seen again.

A Big Box of Hats

Kevin was looking for his roller skates. He looked under his bed. He didn't find his roller skates but he did find a big box. There were some hats inside that Kevin had never seen before.

One of them was a space helmet.

"Excellent!" said Kevin. He loved spacemen. Pulling out the helmet, he put it on.

Whoosh! All of a sudden, Kevin was a spaceman on the Moon. He could see the stars. He was standing by his very own spaceship.

"They must be magic hats!" he thought. "Wow!"

An alien came jumping by. It could jump very high because it was on the Moon. "Floop!" it said.

"Hello!" said Kevin. The alien jumped up and up.

"That looks like fun," said Kevin.

"Floop!" said the alien, jumping again.

Kevin jumped, too. He could jump so high! Six times higher than he could on the Earth.

Then Kevin heard a very loud and anxious "Floop!" from the alien.

The alien had jumped higher still—but this time it hadn't come back down again. It was spinning out of control, away from the Moon!

Kevin jumped as high as he could. He just managed to grab hold of the alien's arm and pull it back down again.

"Floop!" said the alien gratefully.

"Be more careful next time," said Kevin. He went back into his spaceship and closed the door ready for blastoff, then took off his helmet.

Whoosh! Suddenly, Kevin was back in his bedroom. He looked out of the window at the sky.

A spaceship flew across.

"Good-bye, Floop!" said Kevin.

Little Lamb

Little Lamb couldn't sleep,
Not a wink, not a peep!
Tossing, turning, all night through,
What was poor Little Lamb to do?

Owl came by, old and wise,
Said, "Silly lamb, use your eyes—
You're lying in a field of sheep,
Try counting them to help you sleep!"

"Seven, four, thirteen, ten—
That's not right, I'll start again..."
Till daylight came, awake he lay,
And vowed to learn to count next day!

Snow

In the gloom of whiteness,
In the great silence of snow,
A child was sighing
And bitterly saying: "Oh,
They have killed a white bird up there on her nest,
The down is fluttering from her breast!"
And still it fell through that dusky brightness
On the child crying for the bird of the snow.

Birthday Surprise

It was Patch the sheepdog's birthday on Bluebell Farm.

"Fred, it's your job to decorate the barn for the surprise birthday party," said Jenny. "I'm going to bake the cake."

"No problem!" said Farmer Fred.

Farmer Fred sent Patch up to the top field to count sheep, then he and the animals began to decorate the barn. They piled all the presents on a bale of hay and hung up a big banner. Then Farmer Fred started blowing up balloons. He puffed and puffed. It was taking *forever*!

"Never fear, I've got an idea!" he cried, and disappeared into his workshop. Not long after the door swung open and out stepped Farmer Fred pushing a strange-looking machine.

"This," he said proudly, "is the Puffomatic Balloon-blower. All I need to do is flick this switch and we'll have those balloons blown up before you can say *Party Favors*!"

Farmer Fred pulled some balloons over the neck of the machine and flicked a switch. Within seconds the balloons had reached their full size.

"There," said Farmer Fred.

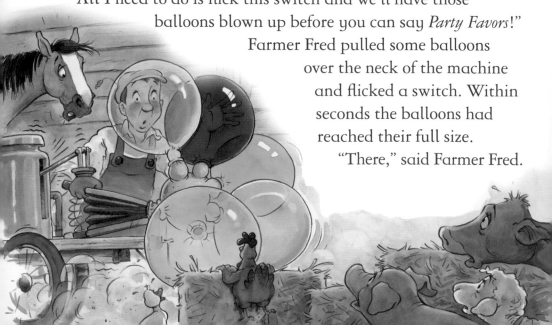

But the Balloon-blower didn't stop. The balloons grew bigger and bigger until suddenly…

BANG! They burst. Bales of hay flew this way and that.

All the animals ran out of the barn as fast as they could.

Patch raced down from the field. "Woof! Woof!" he barked. "What's going on?"

Patch couldn't see Farmer Fred anywhere. He went into the barn. There were bits of machine and bales of hay all over the place. But Farmer Fred was nowhere to be seen.

"Woof! Woof!" barked Patch, as he saw Farmer Fred's hat sticking out from beneath a bale of hay. Patch pushed the bale of hay out of the way. And there was Farmer Fred.

"Woof! Woof!" barked Patch, licking Farmer Fred's face.

"Thanks," laughed Farmer Fred. "I think that perhaps the Puffomatic… err… thingy could do with a bit more work."

Just then, Jenny came into the barn with a bone-shaped cake.

"Ah, you're all here," she smiled, looking around. "And I can see that you've been busy decorating. Now we can start the surprise birthday party."

"Happy Birthday, Patch!" shouted everyone.

I Love Sixpence

I love sixpence, pretty little sixpence,
I love sixpence better than my life;
I spent a penny of it, I spent another,
And I took fourpence home to my wife.

Oh, my little fourpence, pretty little fourpence,
I love fourpence better than my life;
I spent a penny of it, I spent another,
And I took twopence home to my wife.

Oh, my little twopence, my pretty little twopence,
I love twopence better than my life;
I spent a penny of it, I spent another,
And I took nothing home to my wife.

Oh, my little nothing, my pretty little nothing,
What will nothing buy for my wife?
I have nothing, I spend nothing,
I love nothing better than my wife.

From a Train Carriage

Faster than fairies, faster than witches,
Bridges and houses, hedges and ditches;
And charging along like troops in a battle,
All through the meadows the horses and cattle:
All of the sights of the hill and the plain
Fly as thick as driving rain;
And ever again, in the wink of an eye,
Painted stations whistle by.

Here is a child who clambers and scrambles,
All by himself and gathering brambles;
Here is a tramp who stands and gazes;
And there is the green for stringing the daisies!
Here is a cart run away in the road
Lumping along with man and load;
And here is a mill, and there is a river:
Each a glimpse and gone for ever!

Pease Pudding Hot

Pease pudding hot, pease pudding cold,
Pease pudding in the pot, nine days old.
Some like it hot, some like it cold,
Some like it in the pot, nine days old!

Clap Hands

Clap hands for Daddy coming
Down the wagon way,
With a pocketful of money
And a cartload of hay.

Jack and Guy

Jack and Guy went out in the rye,
And they found a little boy with one black eye.
Come, says Jack, let's knock him on the head.
No, says Guy, let's buy him some bread;
You buy one loaf and I'll buy two,
And we'll bring him up as other folk do.

Young Roger Came Tapping

Young Roger came tapping at Dolly's window,
Thumpaty, thumpaty, thump!
He asked for admittance, she answered him "No!"
Frumpaty, frumpaty, frump!

"No, no, Roger, no! As you came you may go!"
Stumpaty, stumpaty, stump!

Five Little Peas

Five little peas in a peapod pressed,
One grew, two grew, and so did all the rest.
They grew, and they grew, and they did not stop,
Until one day the pod went... *Pop!*

Harry Parry

O rare Harry Parry,
When will you marry?
When apples and pears are ripe.
I'll come to your wedding,
Without any bidding,
And dance and sing all the night.

The Science Project

Jed's mom was on the phone. Jed sat at the top of the stairs, listening carefully.

"Mission understood, sir," said Mom. "You can rely on me." She put down the phone and went into the kitchen to finish making dinner.

Jed crept into Mom's office. She had left her work on the computer screen. It told him all about her new mission. Jed smiled.

"Looks like we're going to be busy," he said quietly.

Mom tried to keep her job a secret from Jed, but he knew she was a special agent. A spy! She worked for Unit X, a top-secret organization used by the government to sort out its trickiest problems.

Jed had a secret of his own: he sometimes helped Mom on her missions. But he made sure she never found out.

Jed looked at the computer screen and read about the new mission. An important new invention had disappeared—a new energy-saving fuel. Mom had to find it and return it to the Winger Science Center as soon as possible!

"Dinner's ready, Jed!" Mom called.

Jed turned away from the computer and went downstairs.

"Your favorite!" said Mom, passing him a plateful of chicken curry. "Have you got any homework this weekend?" she asked.

Suddenly, Jed had an idea. "I have a science project on pollution," he replied. "My teacher said the Winger Science Center has a good exhibition. Can we go there, please?" Jed held his breath. Would Mom take the bait?

Mom looked surprised. "What a coincidence!" she said. "I have to visit the Winger Science Center tomorrow afternoon. You can come with me."

The next afternoon, Mom pulled into the Winger Science Center parking lot. "I'll go and talk to the manager while you look at the exhibition," she said. "Meet you in an hour."

"OK," Jed replied. But as Mom walked away, Jed ran off around the side of the building.

Seeing an open window on the ground floor, Jed climbed through it. He found himself in a long corridor. Suddenly he heard a familiar voice. Mom!

Jed quickly hid behind a big potted plant as Mom turned the corner, talking to the research center manager.

"Here's my office," said the manager, opening a door.

Jed breathed a sigh of relief as they disappeared inside.

Mom hadn't seen anything.

Then Jed heard another voice.

"Here, Puss!" it called, from a nearby room.

A large cat hurried past. Jed followed it to a boiler room.

Inside the boiler room, an old caretaker was putting cat food into a bowl. Jed watched from behind the door.

The cat rubbed up against the caretaker, purring loudly.

The caretaker chuckled. "You like this food, don't you, Puss?" he said, as the cat began to eat. "But you don't like that new cat litter, do you?" he added. He looked at a litter tray on the floor. "That stuff's useless!"

He wandered off, muttering, "And whoever heard of *pink* cat litter!"

Jed went over to stroke the cat. He glanced at the cat

litter tray as he passed. Sure enough, it was full of bright pink pellets. How strange.

Jed looked at the label on the sack next to the tray. This was no ordinary cat litter—it was the missing fuel!

"Meow!" yowled the cat.

Jed gave the cat a hurried pat, and then grabbed a handful of the pellets. He made a trail with the pellets from the boiler room to the manager's office.

He glanced at his watch. The hour was nearly up. "Time to go!" he said, running back to the exhibition.

A few minutes later, Jed's mom appeared. She was smiling.

"That was easier than I thought," she said. "Have you found what you wanted, too?"

"Yes thanks, Mom!" Jed replied, smiling back at her.

Hot Cross Buns

Hot cross buns!
Hot cross buns!
One-a-penny, two-a-penny,
Hot cross buns!
If you have no daughters,
Give them to your sons,
One-a-penny, two-a-penny,
Hot cross buns!

Wash Hands

Wash, hands, wash,
Daddy's gone to plow;
If you want your hands wash'd,
Have them wash'd now.

Willie Wastle

I, Willie Wastle,
Stand on my castle,
An' a' the dogs o' your toon,
Will no' drive Willie Wastle down.

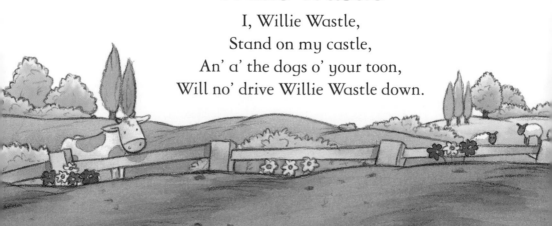

Richard Dick

Richard Dick upon a stick,
Sampson on a sow,
We'll ride away to Colley fair
To buy a horse to plow.

Parliament Soldiers

High diddle ding, did you hear the bells ring?
The parliament soldiers are gone to the king.
Some they did laugh, and some they did cry,
To see the parliament soldiers go by.

Oats and Beans

Oats and beans and barley grow,
Oats and beans and barley grow,
Do you or I or anyone know,
How oats and beans and barley grow?

First the farmer sows his seeds,
Then he stands and takes his ease,
Stamps his feet and claps his hands,
Turns around to view the land.

The Dog and the Ball

It was the summer vacation. Ross and Alexis were camping with their families near the beach.

"Let's play ball on the beach today!" said Alexis.

Ross got a ball from his tent and they went to play on the beach. The sun was shining brightly and the waves were crashing onto the sand.

Ross threw the ball to Alexis. "Catch, Alexis!" he called.

But before Alexis could catch the ball a boy pushed her out of the way and took the ball. He ran off down the beach.

"Hey!" shouted Alexis.

"Come back!" shouted Ross. "That's our ball!"

Ross and Alexis ran after the boy, but they couldn't catch up with him. Soon he had disappeared behind the rocks at the end of the beach.

Then they heard a cry mixed up with some loud barking.

"Help me! Help me!"

"Woof! Woof! Woof!"

Ross and Alexis peered over the rocks. It was the boy who had taken their ball. He was lying on the ground and on top of him was a big, shaggy brown-and-white dog.

"Get him off me," cried the boy. "I'm scared!"

Alexis looked at the dog. Its tail was wagging and its tongue was hanging out. It didn't look scary at all, she thought.

"The dog only wants to play with you, you know," said Alexis.

"Get him off me!" wailed the boy.

"Okay, give me the ball," said Ross to the boy.

The boy gave Ross the ball. Ross leaned back and then threw it far down the beach.

"Fetch!" he called to the dog.

"Woof!" barked the dog excitedly, racing off down the beach after the ball.

The boy jumped up and ran off toward the campsite. He didn't even say thank you.

"What a mean boy," said Alexis.

The dog came racing back with the ball in his mouth. He put it at Ross's feet and waited for Ross to throw it again.

"Never mind," said Ross. "We have our ball."

"And we have a new friend," laughed Alexis, patting the dog.

"Woof!" said the dog.

Jake's First Day

It was Jake Giraffe's first day at school.

"I am too small to go to school, Mom," he said on the way there.

"You're not too small, Jake," said Mom. "Everyone goes to school when they are your age."

"Hello, Jake," said Mrs. Beak, the teacher, when they arrived at school.

"I am too small to go to school, Mrs. Beak," said Jake.

"Why don't you just go inside and have a look?" said Mrs. Beak. "There are a lot of other animals here."

But when Jake tried to go into the school he walked into the door. Bump!

"You are certainly not too small, Jake!" said Mrs. Beak. "You are too tall! We will have to have school outside," she said.

All the other animals came outside.

"This is Jake," said Mrs. Beak.

"Hello, Jake!" they said.

"Hello," said Jake. They looked very friendly.

"We're glad you are here, Jake," said the animals. "School is much more fun outside."

Broken Down

The building site was busy. Digger was busy. Dumper was busy. But Dozer wasn't budging a single inch.

Digger scooped up a big pile of sand. "Come and help, Dozer!" he said.

Dumper tipped out a huge pile of bricks. "Come and help, Dozer!" he said.

But Dozer didn't help. Dozer didn't move even a single inch.

Dumper and Digger were getting annoyed. They had a lot of work to do and they needed Dozer's help.

"Why aren't you helping, Dozer?" asked Digger.

"Have you broken down, Dozer?" asked Dumper.

Digger stopped scooping sand. Dumper stopped tipping bricks. It was very quiet on the building site. Then there was a loud "*Meow…*"

"It's a cat!" said Dozer, proudly.

"*Mew! Mew! Mew!*"

"And her kittens!" said Dozer.

The cat and her kittens had been sound asleep in Dozer's scoop. That was why Dozer wasn't moving. He wasn't being lazy and he hadn't broken down.

"The kittens are safe," smiled Dozer.

A Jittery Journey

The moon's like a wizard's face up in the sky,
The night is as black as a cat.
The trees' branches rustle and wave as you pass,
Then reach down to snatch off your hat.

The wind wants to whisper a secret to you,
An owl hoots, "Noo! Noo! Shouldn't tell!"
You can hear a dog howling (or is it a wolf?)
And the chimes of a distant church bell.

A monster is lying in wait by the path—
With hundreds of feet and big teeth!
Or is it a tree fallen, struck in a storm,
With toadstools growing beneath?

Quick! Is that a light you can see through the wood?
Hurry up, there are bats flying around!
Here you are at the gate—Mom opens the door,
And you're home once again—safe and sound!

It's Raining

It's raining cats and dogs,
And warty toads and frogs,
And red-kneed bats and bowler hats.
It's raining big fat hogs.

It's raining needles and pins,
And rusty cans and tins,
And things I don't like—such as bits of bike.
It's raining violins.

It's raining apples and pears,
And dolls and teddy bears,
And silly pigs in curly wigs.
It's raining plastic chairs.

It's raining bacon and eggs,
And laundry lines and pegs,
And cowboy suits and exotic fruits.
It's raining hairy legs.

It's raining ducks and drakes,
And chocolate bars and cakes,
And glasses of milk and colorful silk.
It's raining garden rakes.

Missing Milk

One day, Farmer Fred was feeling very pleased with himself.

"I'm not one to boast," he told his wife Jenny, "but I'm sure my singing is doing Connie Cow a world of good. She's grown very plump around the middle. And she's giving me buckets of milk."

Jenny looked at Connie. "Do you suppose she could be…?"

But Farmer Fred was too busy singing to listen.

The next day, as Connie waddled toward the milking shed, the other farm animals gossiped among themselves.

"I'm sure she's getting fatter," clucked Hetty Hen.

"You don't suppose that she's having a baby, do you?" asked Harry Horse. The animals began to chatter excitedly among themselves.

A week later, Farmer Fred wasn't feeling so pleased.

"Connie's run out of milk," he moaned. "Perhaps I'm singing the wrong songs." He closed his eyes and burst into song. Connie mooed loudly. She wished Farmer Fred could be quieter.

"I just don't understand it," said Farmer Fred. "Where has her milk gone?"

The animals tried to tell Farmer Fred that Connie had a new calf who was drinking all Connie's milk. But Farmer Fred just looked puzzled at all the noise.

"He just doesn't understand," sighed Harry Horse, knocking over the bucket with his hoof. Farmer Fred's eyes lit up.

"Yes, that's got to be it! We've got a milk thief on the farm!" cried Farmer Fred. "But never fear, I've got an idea!"

Farmer Fred disappeared into his workshop. There were sounds of drawers opening and closing, and cabinet doors banging.

All the animals watched on, wondering what was happening.

"What's Farmer Fred up to now?" asked Polly Pig.

Finally, Farmer Fred came out holding a large ball of string that he had found.

"I'm going to set a trap to catch that milk thief," he said. Farmer Fred got a really long piece of string and tied one end to the gate leading to Cowslip Meadow.

When Farmer Fred went to bed that night, he tied the other end of the string to his big toe.

He had only been sleeping for a few minutes when he felt a tugging on his big toe.

"Thundering turnips!" grunted Farmer Fred, hopping out of bed.

He peered through the window. But it was only an

only an owl perching on the string.

"Get off my string!" he shouted.

Soon there was so much noise that everyone woke up.

The next morning, everyone on the farm was very, very tired. Hetty Hen called a farmyard meeting. Everyone but Connie was there.

"It's time Farmer Fred found out the truth about Connie. Otherwise we'll never get any peace around here," yawned Hetty Hen.

"Patch, it's up to you," neighed Harry Horse. "Farmer Fred always listens to you."

That night, Farmer Fred stood guard with his pitchfork in Cowslip Meadow.

"No one's going to get away with stealing my milk," he muttered.

Very slowly, and very carefully, he began counting the cows.

"One, two, yawn…" All this counting was making him sleepy. "Three, four, yawn… zzzz." He was fast asleep before he'd even reached five. But Patch wasn't going to let Farmer Fred snooze the night away.

"Woof, woof!" he barked.

"What? Where?" cried Farmer Fred, suddenly waking up.

"Woof, woof!" Patch set off through the field barking over

his shoulder at Farmer Fred.

"Do you want me to follow you, Patch?" asked Farmer Fred sleepily. "Have you found that milk thief?"

Patch led Farmer Fred to the old barn at the top of the field.

Farmer Fred shone his flashlight around the barn. And there in the corner was Connie. Beside her was the milk thief—a beautiful baby calf.

"Aah! You've got a little calf to feed!" cried Farmer Fred. "No wonder you had no milk to spare, Connie!"

The next day, Farmer Fred was feeling very pleased with himself.

"I'm not one to boast," Farmer Fred told Jenny, "but I just knew Connie was going to have a calf. After all, she was looking very plump!"

Jenny and Patch looked at each other and rolled their eyes.

Harry, Hetty, Polly, Shirley, and all the other animals smiled happily. Now, perhaps, they could all get some sleep!

Without a Growl

When Old MacDonald's work is done,
And twilight falls with the setting sun,
He sits down in his chair.
For he knows that he has a friend,
From day's beginning to day's end,
Bruce the sheepdog is there.

Bread and Milk for Breakfast

Bread and milk for breakfast,
And woollen frocks to wear,
And a crumb for robin redbreast
On the cold days of the year.

Old Joe Brown

Old Joe Brown, he had a wife,
She was all of eight feet tall.
She slept with her head in the kitchen,
And her feet stuck out in the hall.

Robert Rowley

Robert Rowley rolled a round roll round,
A round roll Robert Rowley rolled round;
Where rolled the round roll Robert Rowley rolled round?

Old John Muddlecombe

Old John Muddlecombe lost his cap,
He couldn't find it anywhere, the poor old chap.
He walked down the High Street, and everybody said,
"Silly John Muddlecombe, you've got it on your head!"

There Was a King

There was a king, and he had three daughters,
And they all lived in a basin of water;
The basin's bended,
My story's ended.
If the basin had been stronger,
My story would have been longer.

The Dragon's Cave

One fine sunny day, Sir Sam the Small was riding past a little village. He was just thinking about what to have for lunch when the whole village came running out to meet him.

"A knight!" they shouted. "A knight!"

"That's right!" said Sir Sam, jumping down from his horse. "How can I help you?"

"There's a dragon living on top of the hill," a lady said. "We're afraid of him! His cave smokes night and day and we're scared that soon he'll get hungry and come down and eat us!"

"You're a knight. Can you save us from the dragon?" added a man.

"I'll certainly try," said Sir Sam.

Sir Sam went to the dragon's cave on top of the hill. The people were right. There were clouds of smoke coming from the cave. He took out his sword.

"Come out, dragon!" Sam called. "Come out and fight!"

The dragon came out. Now, Sir Sam had fought a lot of dragons. Big dragons. Fierce dragons. Dragons who would gobble up a village for breakfast, and then follow up with a town for lunch. This dragon didn't look very big or very scary.

"I just burned my toast," said the dragon to Sir Sam, grumpily. "Bother. I'm always doing that."

"The people in the village below are afraid of you, you know," said Sir Sam.

The dragon looked astonished. "Are they?" he asked. "Why on earth are they afraid of me?"

"It's the clouds of smoke," said Sir Sam. "I know, why don't you invite them to lunch this afternoon? Then you can make friends."

"Great idea!" said the dragon.

Sir Sam went down to the village and told the people about the dragon. "He just wants to be friends," he said. "And he's invited you all to lunch this afternoon."

Everyone went up to the dragon's cave. The dragon was delighted to see them. "Have some toast!" he said.

Sir Sam looked at the toast. It was very, very black.

"I think I'll stick to cakes, thanks," he said.

I Love You, Daddy

"You're getting tall, Little Bear," said Daddy Bear. "Big enough to come climbing with me."

Little Bear's eyes opened wide in surprise.

"Do you really mean that?" said Little Bear.

Daddy Bear nodded. He led Little Bear to a giant tree.

Little Bear tried to scramble up onto the lowest branch. He tumbled backward.

Daddy Bear tugged Little Bear.

"You can do it!" he whispered.

And suddenly, Little Bear found that he could.

"I love Daddy," thought Little Bear.

"You're getting brave, Little Bear," said Daddy Bear. "Daring enough to gather honey."

Little Bear gasped. "Could I really?"

Daddy Bear winked. He led Little Bear to another tree and pointed to a hole in the trunk. Little Bear reached out his paw. A furious buzzing filled his ears. Little Bear pulled his paw back.

"Just be quick," Daddy Bear said. "You have thick fur. The bees can't hurt you. You can do it!" he smiled.

And suddenly, Little Bear found that he could.

"I love Daddy," thought Little Bear.

"You're getting smart, Little Bear. Smart enough to find a good winter den," said Daddy.

Little Bear grinned. "Do you really think so?"

"I know so," said Daddy Bear.

Little Bear set off. "Not too far from food," said Daddy Bear. "Ready for when spring comes."

Little Bear sniffed the wind.

"Look for high ground," said Daddy Bear, "to keep us dry." "Somewhere safe and warm and away from danger."

"Here!" called Little Bear as he disappeared into a deep cave.

Daddy Bear followed. He looked all around. "Perfect! Well done, Little Bear!"

"I love Daddy," thought Little Bear.

"Did I climb well?" Little Bear asked on the way home.

"You did!" replied Daddy Bear.

"Was I brave when I got the honey from the bees' nest?" asked Little Bear.

"You were!" answered Daddy Bear.

"Did I find a good den?" asked Little Bear.

"The very best!" smiled Daddy Bear.

Suddenly, Little Bear felt very tired, but there was something he wanted to say.

"I love you, D..." began Little Bear. But he didn't finish.

Daddy Bear gently lifted Little Bear onto his back and began the long journey home. "I love you, too," he whispered.

Marching Band

Oompah, oompah goes the trombone,
Held tight in a bony hand.
Boom, boom, boom the bass drum thunders.
Meet the Monster Marching Band!

Ghoulish fingers clutch at drumsticks,
Zombies march past with glazed eyes,
Vampires play on tuneless tubas,
Mummies blow horns to the skies.

A spectral player sounds the bugle,
Ghastly ghosts play clarinets,
On they march past church and graveyard,
Led by phantom majorettes!

So if you ever chance to hear them,
Marching through the town at night,
Just stay put beneath your covers,
Or you'll be in for a fright!

A Good Play

We built a ship upon the stairs
All made of the back-bedroom chairs,
And filled it full of sofa pillows
To go a-sailing on the billows.

We took a saw and several nails,
And water in the nursery pails;
And Tom said, "Let us also take
An apple and a slice of cake;"
Which was enough for Tom and me
To go a-sailing on the sea.

We sailed along for days and days,
And had the very best of plays;
But Tom fell out and hurt his knee,
So there was no one left but me.

Hide-and-seek

It was playtime at school. The animals were playing hide-and-seek. Lucy Lion counted to ten. The animals ran to hide.

"Ninety-nine... One hundred! I'm coming!" called Lucy.

Lucy looked high and low. She couldn't find Helga Hippo.

Lucy looked high and low. She couldn't find Mikey Monkey.

Lucy looked high and low. She couldn't find Jake Giraffe.

"Where is everybody?" Lucy wondered. She kept looking. She looked and looked and looked until she started to get tired.

When the bell rang for the end of playtime the animals came out of their hiding places.

"Where's Lucy?" asked Mrs. Beak, the teacher.

They looked high and low for Lucy. Helga Hippo couldn't find her. Mikey Monkey couldn't find her. Jake Giraffe couldn't find her.

Then Mrs. Beak found her. Lucy had given up. She was fast asleep under a tree!

Smasher Can

Dozer was busy moving sand. Digger was busy scooping. Dumper was busy tipping. They were building a house.

Michael the builder was securing the roof. He had climbed up there using a ladder.

"Look out!" said Digger.

"Look out!" said Dozer.

Dumper wasn't looking where he was going. He bumped into the ladder. *Crash!* The ladder fell down.

"Help!" said Michael. He was stuck on the roof.

"I can't reach," said Dumper.

"I can't reach," said Digger.

"I can't reach, either," said Dozer.

"I know who can reach," said Dumper. "Smasher can!" Smasher was a crane.

Very carefully, Smasher swung his big metal ball toward Michael. Michael climbed onto it. Then Smasher lowered the ball down to the ground.

"Thanks, Smasher!" grinned Michael, putting his ladder back up.

"Sorry, Michael," said Dumper. "I'll look where I'm going next time."

The Lost Valley

Deep in the steamy jungle there was a secret valley that had lain undisturbed since life on Earth began.

A few local people knew about the valley, but they kept far away. Stories had been told that terrifying beasts prowled through the lush forests. And it was true—something terrifying did lurk in that valley. For in it lived the last Diplodocus dinosaurs in the world.

One day, a circus owner called Terrible Tony heard about the valley, while tracking down magnificent wild animals for his traveling circus.

"With any luck," he thought, his eyes glinting wickedly, "the monster will be some kind of dangerous animal that will earn me loads of money!" He was determined to find the valley.

Tony armed himself with stun guns, giant nets, and even a lasso. He stocked up with provisions and set sail down the river in an inflatable raft.

The further Tony traveled into the jungle, the wilder it became.

One morning, the ground began to shudder. The trees parted and a giant creature burst out of the jungle. It was as long as a town square.

If Tony had had any sense, he would have run for his life. Instead he yelled, "Over here!"

The Diplodocus couldn't hear him. Tony's shouts sounded like tiny, faraway squeaks. However, it had seen the bright orange raft and made straight for it.

Tony fired a round of darts from his stun gun at the huge creature and waited for it to keel over.

The Diplodocus just shook itself lazily and looked a little bit annoyed. It studied the tiny red-faced man that was irritating it, then bent down and seized Tony in its mouth.

But the Diplodocus, being a plant eater, didn't eat Tony. Instead, it tossed him away. Then it picked up the raft and hurled it after him.

Tony flew out of the valley and over the hills beyond.

Luckily for him, he landed safely, with an almighty splash, in a distant lagoon.

A few moments later, his raft hit the water right beside him. Tony paddled across that lagoon to the town on its banks as fast as he could go. Then he hailed a taxi to the airport, boarded a plane, and never, ever went back to the valley.

Meeting the Diplodocus changed Tony forever. He shut down his circus and released all the animals safely back into the wild.

And the herd of Diplodocus lived happily ever after.

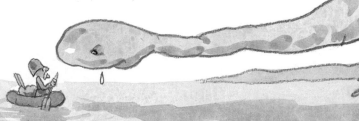

Lonely Whale

"I wish I had someone to play with," said Whale. He was splashing around by himself in the ocean.

"Hello, Whale! Want to play?" asked Seahorse, jumping out from under the rocks. But Seahorse was so small, Whale didn't hear him.

Two dolphins began leaping to and fro across Whale's back. "Play with us, Whale!" they cried. But Whale was so big, he didn't notice them.

Then three fish floated by. "Play with us, Whale!" they said. But the fish were so far away, Whale didn't see them.

Whale found Eel wriggling around the rocks. "I'd like to wriggle like that," said Whale. "But I'm so big and clumsy, I can't do anything," said Whale, sadly.

"But you're the biggest animal in the ocean. Everyone loves you," said Eel. "Have a look behind you!"

Whale turned around and saw all the fish in the ocean!

"Please play, Whale," they cried.

"I'm the luckiest whale in the whole world!" said Whale, and he swam off to join his friends.

Ssssh!

It was the middle of the night. All of a
sudden, Kitten's tummy began to rumble.

"I'm really hungry!" said Kitten. "I've
just got to go to the kitchen and find
something to eat."

Kitten tried to quietly jump to the
floor, but he landed on Puppy's tail instead.

"*Ow!*" cried Puppy.

"*Ssssh!*" whispered Kitten. "You'll
wake everyone up!"

Kitten tiptoed down the hall…

"*Boo!*" shouted Rabbit, hopping up.

"*Ssssh!*" whispered Kitten. "You'll wake
everyone up!"

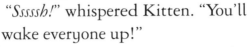

Kitten crept through the living room and
was startled by a noise under the sofa.

"Who's there?" asked Kitten, nervously.

"*Squeak! Squeak!*" squeaked Hamster.

"*Sssshh!*" whispered Kitten. "You'll wake everyone up!"

"*Meeeow!*" howled Kitten when he reached the kitchen at
last. There was a fat little mouse eating out of his bowl!

Crash! went the bowl, and the dishes, and the saucepans, as
Kitten chased the mouse all over the kitchen.

And after all that loud noise, who do you think woke up?
Everyone!

The Shopping Trip

"I wish I could buy a new bike," said David, gazing into the bike store window. "Mine's useless."

"Me too," said Josh. "But neither of us has any money."

They both sighed.

David grabbed Josh's arm. "I know!" he said. "We could make our own money running errands!"

"Try Mrs. Cole next door," said David's mom, when they told her their plan. "She might have a few jobs you could do."

Mrs. Cole gave David and Josh a huge shopping list. "Make sure you don't forget anything!" she snapped. Mrs. Cole was always bad tempered.

David and Josh spent ages at the grocery store finding everything on the list. They paid at the checkout and stared at the pile of heavy bags.

"How are we going to carry all this?" Josh asked.

"Wait here!" David told Josh. And he raced off.

David returned with his baby sister's stroller and Rusty, his dog.

"Put the groceries in the stroller, Josh," he said, tying
Rusty's leash to the stroller. "Rusty can pull the stroller home
for us."

But as Josh put the last bag in the stroller, Rusty saw a cat
and darted after it.

"Quick!" yelled David. "Follow that stroller!"

As Rusty and the stroller passed Mrs. Cole's house, Rusty
dodged a lamppost and *Crash!* The stroller smashed right
into it.

Five big grocery bags flew through the air and then landed
with a terrible clatter.

Mrs. Cole rushed out. "Clean up this mess!" she shouted.
"And then buy me some more groceries with your own money!"
She marched back into her house and slammed the door.

Then a window opened. It was Mr. Cole. "That chase was
the funniest thing!" he said, laughing. "Come over here."

The boys went over to the window. "Don't tell Mrs. Cole I
paid you," he whispered, handing them the money. "And don't
worry about the cost of the groceries, either. Seeing something
so funny was worth it!"

Poor Old Robinson Crusoe!

Poor old Robinson Crusoe!
Poor old Robinson Crusoe!
They made him a coat of an old nanny goat,
I wonder how they could do so!
With a ring a ting tang,
And a ring a ting tang,
Poor old Robinson Crusoe!

Jack Sprat

Jack Sprat could eat no fat,
His wife could eat no lean,
And so between the two of them
They licked the platter clean.

Rub-a-Dub Dub

Rub-a-dub dub, three men in a tub,
And who do you think they be?
The butcher, the baker, the candlestick maker,
Turn them out knaves all three.

Solomon Grundy

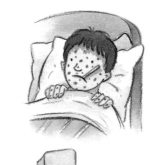

Solomon Grundy,
Born on Monday,
Christened on Tuesday,
Married on Wednesday,
Sick on Thursday,
Worse on Friday,
Died on Saturday,
Buried on Sunday,
That was the end
Of Solomon Grundy.

Me, Myself, and I

Me, myself, and I—
We went to the kitchen and ate a pie.
Then my mother she came in
And chased us out with a rolling pin.

Swan Swam Over the Sea

Swan swam over the ocean—
Swim, swan, swim,
Swan swam back again,
Well swum swan.

Tent Trouble

Ross and Alexis were on the swings in the campsite playground.

"This is great!" said Ross, pushing off as hard as he could.

Jaden and Kim, who were staying in the tent next door to Ross and Alexis, were watching.

"Swings are for babies," said Jaden.

"It's fun," said Alexis.

"We're going to have better fun," said Jaden.

"What are you going to do?" asked Ross.

"We're not telling you," said Kim. And they ran off.

"I wonder what they're going to do?" said Alexis.

"Let's follow them," said Ross.

Ross and Alexis followed Jaden and Kim across the campsite back to where their tents were pitched.

From behind the bushes, they watched Jaden and Kim pulling out all the tent pegs in their parents' tent one by one

and laughing.

"Now this is fun!" Jaden was saying to Kim.

"The tent is going to fall down!" said Alexis.

"Look out!" shouted Ross, as loudly as he could.

Jaden's mom and dad

looked out of the tent...
just as it fell down around
their ears with a huge
flapping noise!

"Ouch!" cried Jaden
and Kim's dad, as a pole
hit him on the head.

Jaden and Kim's parents
crawled out of the ruined
tent.

"I wonder what
happened?" said Jaden and
Kim's dad. "We must have not put it up properly."

Jaden and Kim were trying hard not to giggle.

Ross stepped out from behind the bushes.

"It wasn't the wind," he said. "Jaden and Kim pulled out all
the tent pegs."

"Jaden! Kim!" shouted
their parents.

"It was a joke!" said
Jaden.

"I have a better joke,"
said their mom. She picked
up the tent pegs and gave
them to Jaden and Kim.

"Put the tent back up!"
she said.

The Royal Mystery

"Jed, go and clean your room!" shouted Mom. She was in a really bad mood.

"But it is clean!" Jed protested, stomping upstairs. "Maybe she's having trouble with a mission," he said to himself. "I'd better check what she's up to."

While Mom was in the shower, Jed took a look at her computer screen. Jed's mom was a spy for government agency Unit X. What she didn't know was that Jed sometimes helped out secretly with some of her missions.

"The state governor has been disappearing from her house every night," he read. "The government thinks she may be working as a spy. Your mission is to find out what she is doing."

Jed went back to his bedroom. He would follow Mom to work that evening.

Jed put a pillow under his comforter to make Elise the babysitter think he was asleep if she looked in on him. Then he turned out the light, opened his window, and climbed out. He hid in the shadows, waiting for Mom to leave the house.

A few moments later, Mom came out and began to walk down the street. Jed followed her. After a bus ride and a long walk, she stopped outside a huge house.

"That must be the governor's mansion," Jed said to himself.

Mom's cell phone rang. As she talked on the phone, she didn't notice a shadowy figure leave the house through a side door.

Jed watched. It was a woman wearing sunglasses—even though it was dark. Jed guessed it must be the governor.

Jed left his mom chatting and followed the governor down a half-hidden little alley. At the end of it was another street with a lot of stores and restaurants.

Jed watched as the governor slipped into Jimmy's Burger Joint. He hurried in after her.

"What will you have tonight, my dear?" the man behind the counter asked the governor.

"My favorite burger and fries, please, Jimmy!" said the governor, cheerfully. "It's such a pity they never serve it at the banquets I go to. That's why I come here!"

Smiling, Jed slipped out of the restaurant and went home. The next evening was Mom's night off.

"Can we go out to eat tonight?" Jed asked her.

Mum sighed. "I don't feel like cooking, so that's fine by me," she said gloomily.

"I want a burger and fries," said Jed. "And I heard about a really great place in town. It's called Jimmy's Burger Joint."

At Jimmy's, Jed and Mom sat down to eat their burgers.

A few minutes later, in walked the governor.

Mom nearly choked on a fry.

"Hello, my dear. How lovely to see you again!" said Jimmy to the governor.

"I just can't keep away from your delicious food, Jimmy," said the governor with a smile. "Now let me think—I'll have my usual burger and fries, please!"

As Jed's mom looked at the governor eating her burger she smiled for the first time in days.

"I'm very glad we went out to eat, Jed," she said. "This was an excellent place to come!"

Jed nodded happily.

"Another mystery solved!" he thought.

The Singing Bank Robber

Christopher McTavish had been having a bad day at the office. He sent his last e-mail of the day, sighed, and put on his leather motorcycle gear. He'd accidentally left the sports bag he usually put his office clothes in at home that morning, so he found an empty bag in the safe and used that instead.

Then he started for home. He hadn't gone very far when the motorcycle coughed, juddered, and stopped.

With another deep sigh, Christopher dismounted, tucked his helmet under his arm, and trudged home. It started to rain.

"How was your day, Dad?" called his son, Jamie.

"Awful," said Christopher.

Just then there was a loud, insistent knock at the door, and a gruff voice said, "Open up! We know you're in there!"

Christopher and Jamie McTavish looked nervously at each other, then Christopher opened the door. There were two stern-looking policemen on the doorstep.

"We have been trailing you, sir," said the first one, "and we have reason to believe that you are the man who robbed the bank in the main street this afternoon."

"Me?" cried Christopher.

"You fit the description perfectly, sir. Leathers, slicked-back hair, and large bag of cash."

"That was my suit," said

Christopher. "And my hair isn't slicked back, it's wet. I got caught in a shower."

"So how do you explain the bowling ball?" said the policeman. "The robber threatened to knock out the bank manager with a bowling ball. You had a bowling ball tucked under your arm, sir."

"Oh, no," said Christopher. "That's not a bowling ball. That's my motorcycle helmet."

"Ah-ha!" said the policeman. "But you arrived here on foot."

"Yes, my bike broke down," said Christopher. "There's an explanation for everything."

The first policeman whispered something to the second policeman then said, "Could you sing for us, sir?"

Christopher was beginning to think these two policemen were completely mad. He took a deep breath and started to sing. It sounded terrible. Christopher had never been much of a singer.

"Well, that's it," said the second policeman. "This is the wrong guy. He isn't the bank robber."

"Why?" asked a bewildered Jamie.

"Well, an eyewitness said the robber was singing something from an opera. And he sounded very good. So this man can't possibly be him. Sorry to have bothered you."

"My singing's not that bad," said Christopher, offended.

"Yes it is, Dad!" said Jamie.

One Dark Night

Paws tiptoed out into the dark farmyard. Mommy had told him to stay in the barn until he was old enough to go out at night, but he was impatient.

"*Hoot! Hoot! Hoot!*" Loud hoots echoed through the trees, and a great dark shape swooped down and snatched something up.

"Just an owl," Paws told himself, creeping nervously on into the darkness. "Nothing to be afraid of!"

Strange rustlings came from every corner.

Oink! Paws jumped. But it was just the old pig in the pigpen close by.

Then, all of a sudden, Paws froze in his tracks. Beneath the hen house two eyes glinted in the darkness. They came creeping toward him… this must be the fox Mommy had warned him about! But then, to his amazement, he saw it was Mommy!

"Back to the barn!" she said sternly. And Paws happily did as he was told. Maybe he would wait until he was older to go out at night, after all!

Naughty Duckling

Mommy Duck is in a flap.
"My naughty duckling won't come back!"

She's off to chase him, on his tail—
Following Little Duckling's trail.

"Go over the hill!" the little foal neighs,
"I saw Little Duckling run that way!"

"Along the fence!" baby calf moos,
"You'll catch him if you hurry, too!"

The piglets oink, "We saw him slide!
Up on the roof and down the side!"

"Look under here!" the lambs all baa,
"He can't have gone so very far!"

"He came past here!" cheeps little chick,
"He said hello, then ran off, quick!"

And there he is! He loves to roam.
But most of all he loves his home!

Tiger Footprints

It was a very hot day in the jungle. Tiggy and Mac were playing near the waterfall.

"Wheee!" shouted Tiggy, as she slid on the wet rocks.

Mac was watching a funny-looking frog. It croaked loudly and then hopped away.

"Where are you going?" asked Mac.

When the little frog didn't answer, Mac ran after it.

"Wait for me!" cried Tiggy.

The twins chased the frog through the leafy jungle.

"Look!" shouted Mac suddenly.

Tiggy tumbled to a stop behind him. In front of them sat a whole family of funny-looking frogs.

"The little frog was hopping back home," said Mac.

Tiggy was tired after their long chase. "I want to go home," she groaned.

Mac looked around. They had never been here before. He didn't know how to get home.

"I wish Mom were here," sighed Mac. "She always knows the way home."

As the two cubs looked around, Tiggy noticed a trail of footprints on the soft jungle floor. The footprints were round

—and very big.

"Maybe they'll lead us home," said Mac.

The little tigers followed them carefully, and at the end, they came across a baby elephant.

"This isn't home," said Tiggy. And the two cubs ran away as fast as their little legs could carry them. Finally, the little tigers had run far enough and they stopped for a rest.

"Look! We've made a trail, too," said Mac.

The pair looked back at the footprints that followed them.

"Let's make some more," cried Tiggy. And they ran faster and faster, making a zigzagging trail of tiger footprints.

Then Tiggy noticed some more footprints nearby.

"Those look just like ours," she said, "but much bigger."

"Mom!" they both shouted together.

And the little cubs began to follow the big tiger footprints back through the leafy jungle to where...

... Mom stood waiting.

"Come on, you two little tigers," she said, smiling at her cubs. "Time to go home!"

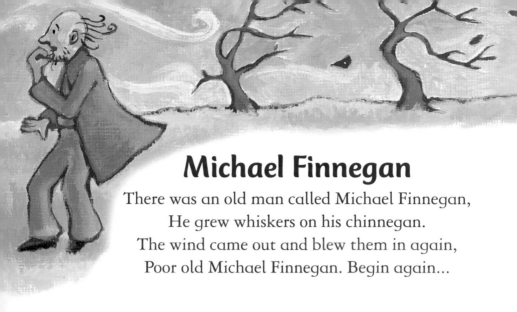

Michael Finnegan

There was an old man called Michael Finnegan,
He grew whiskers on his chinnegan.
The wind came out and blew them in again,
Poor old Michael Finnegan. Begin again...

There Was a Man

There was a man, and his name was Dob,
And he had a wife, and her name was Mob,
And he had a dog, and he called it Cob,
And she had a cat, called Chitterabob.
Cob, says Dob,
Chitterabob, says Mob,
Cob was Dob's dog,
Chitterabob Mob's cat.

Hey, Dorolot, Dorolot!

Hey, dorolot, dorolot!
Hey, dorolay, dorolay!
Hey, my bonny boat, bonny boat,
Hey, drag away, drag away!

Adam and Eve and Pinchme

Adam and Eve and Pinchme
Went down to the river to bathe.
Adam and Eve were drowned—
Who do you think was saved?

Peter Piper

Peter Piper picked a peck of pickled pepper;
A peck of pickled pepper Peter Piper picked;
If Peter Piper picked a peck of pickled pepper,
Where's the peck of pickled pepper Peter Piper picked?

My Hands

My hands upon my head I place,
On my shoulders, on my face;
On my hips I place them so,
Then bend down to touch my toe.

Now I raise them up so high,
Make my fingers fairly fly,
Now I clap them, one, two, three.
Then I fold them silently.

The Farm Show

Farmer Jones was very excited. It was the day of the Sunnybridge Farm Show.

Mrs. Jones was entering the Jam-making Competition, and Farmer Jones was entering almost everything else.

"Perhaps you should just enter one thing," said Mrs. Jones.

"But there are so many prizes to win," laughed Farmer Jones. "How could I possibly choose? Right, Max?"

Max, Farmer Jones' sheepdog, wagged his tail. He was looking forward to the Farm Show, too.

"Polly is sure to win the Prettiest Pig," said Farmer Jones, as he and Max made their way to the pigpen where Polly lived.

But Polly had been rolling in something very dirty and very smelly.

"Phwah!" gasped Farmer Jones.

"Woof!" barked Max, running back to the farmhouse to fetch some of Mrs. Jones' extra-strong laundry soap. Farmer Jones used the soap to make a bath.

But it was no good.

Polly was just too dirty and too smelly. They would never get her clean in time.

"Double bother! It doesn't look like I'll be winning the prize for the Prettiest Pig this year," said Farmer Jones. "But Bonnie is sure to win the prize for the Whitest Lamb."

Farmer Jones borrowed some of Mrs. Jones' best shampoo and made a bath for Bonnie.

"In you go!" he said, plonking Bonnie into the tub. Farmer Jones began to scrub away. He closed his eyes and began to sing:

"Oh, what a beautiful morning!
Oh, what a beautiful day!
I have a wonderful feeling
I'll win some prizes today!"

"Woof!" barked Max. He tugged at Farmer Jones' sleeve.

"What is it?" asked Farmer Jones.

But it was too late. Bonnie was bright pink.

Farmer Jones had picked up Mrs. Jones' hair dye instead of shampoo!

"Bother!" said Farmer Jones. "It doesn't look like I'll be winning the prize for the Whitest Lamb this year. But Chloe is sure to win the prize for the Smartest Cow."

Max fetched Chloe from the meadow. Farmer Jones tied her up and found a brush.

"We'll soon have you gleaming," said Farmer Jones. But Chloe had other ideas. As soon as the brush touched her side, she began to wriggle and squirm.

Farmer Jones had forgotten that Chloe was ticklish! Chloe would not stand still. She would never be ready in time.

"Botheration!" said Farmer Jones. "Now what am I going to do?"

"Are you ready?" shouted Mrs. Jones from the farmhouse. "I don't want to be late for the Jam-making Competition."

"Double botheration!" said Farmer Jones. "I've run out of time. It doesn't look like I'll be entering any of the competitions this year."

Later, at Sunnybridge Farm Show, Mrs. Jones won first prize in the Jam-making Competition.

Farmer Jones watched as other farmers won the rest

of the competitions, one by one.

"Oh, if only I could enter just one little competition," said Farmer Jones.

"Woof!" barked Max. He ran around in circles, pretending to round up some invisible animals.

Suddenly, Farmer Jones understood. "Of course! The Sheepdog Competition," he said.

A few minutes later, they were in the ring. Farmer Jones whistled and Max herded the sheep this way and that. The sheep were herded into the pen in record time.

"And the winners are Farmer Jones and Max," said a voice over the loud speaker. The crowd clapped and cheered.

Later, Farmer Jones showed Mrs. Jones the shiny trophy they had won.

"It's like I always say," said Farmer Jones happily. "It's best to concentrate on just one thing."

Mrs. Jones peered over the cup she had won for her jam.

"Yes, dear," she said, winking.

The White Feather

Duck was waddling around the farmyard, when
she saw a large white feather floating in the
pond. She fished it out with her beak, and
put it in her tail.

But when Pig saw Duck, he burst out
laughing. "You look so silly!" he cried,
rolling around in the mud.

"I thought I looked pretty," said Duck,
feeling a bit sad.

Duck went to find Horse. "Do I look silly
with my nice new feather?" she asked him.

"I think you look wonderful!" said Horse,
kindly. "But that feather isn't yours. It belongs to Chicken."

"Then I'll give it back at once," said Duck. She went
straight to see Chicken. "I've got your feather," said Duck.
"I'm so sorry."

"Thank you!" cried Chicken,
putting the feather back in her own
tail, where it looked just perfect.

"And how beautiful you look
with your fine yellow feathers,
Duck," she said.

Duck waddled out into the
farmyard feeling very pretty
indeed!

Lost Bananas

One day, Elephant was stomping through the jungle when she found a huge bunch of bananas lying under a tree. "Someone must have lost these," she thought. "I'll go and ask Snake."

Elephant found Snake sunbathing on a rock. "Have you lost these bananas, Snake?" asked Elephant.

"How deliciousssss! But they're not my bananassss!" hissed Snake, and slithered into the trees.

"I'll just leave them here, then," said Elephant. "Someone will find them." And she plodded back into the jungle.

A giraffe with a long, thin neck came swaying past, and saw the bananas sitting on the rock.

"What a pity! Someone has lost their dinner," she said, bending down to eat the thick jungle grass.

"Someone must want those bananas!" said Parrot, watching from a tree.

Suddenly she heard a rustling in the branches...

... and a troupe of monkeys came swinging through the trees!

"Of course! Monkeys love eating bananas!" cried Parrot.

"Wow, what a fantastic bunch of bananas!" said the monkeys. "Let's have a *huge* jungle feast! Come on everybody! Let's eat!"

There Was an Old Lady

There was an old lady
Who lived down our street,
You wouldn't believe all
The things she could eat.

For breakfast each morning,
A full three-course meal
Of nuts and bolts served in
A bicycle wheel!

She always took care
To never miss lunch,
On brooms, mops, and buckets
She'd nibble and crunch.

Trumpets and trombones were
Her favorite dinner,
But though always eating,
She kept getting thinner.

Finally, for supper she'd snack on
Some bees in their hives,
All swiftly washed down with
The forks, spoons, and knives!

Did You Ever See...

Did you ever see a jester juggling with ice creams,
Or a pair of giant hamsters wrestling in your dreams?
If you've never seen a crocodile swallow twenty conkers,
Then you, my friend, are honestly quite bonkers!

Did you ever see a puppy dancing with an umbrella,
Or a sweet old lady who thought she was Cinderella?
If you've never seen an elephant sitting on a daisy,
Then you, my friend, are honestly quite crazy!

Did you ever see a singing worm climbing up a wall,
Or a judge stand up in court, and catch a basketball?
If you've never seen a kangaroo asleep in silk pajamas,
Then you, my friend, are honestly quite bananas!

I know people think I'm nuts—but here's my explanation:
I make up loads of stuff with my wild imagination!

Treasure Map

Captain Diamond and her band of ruthless pirates were very excited. They were on the hunt for treasure!

Captain Diamond showed them all the treasure map. There was an "X" marked on it. It was six steps from a rock.

"There'll be gold doubloons and silver sovereigns, rubies red as blood, sapphires bluer than the sky, and diamonds worth more than this entire ship!" she said.

Billy the cabin boy was as excited as everyone else. "I'd really like a gold doubloon," he thought. "Just one." But he didn't think that he'd be allowed any of the treasure. He was too young.

The pirates landed on the beach. "Come on, me hearties!" cried Diamond, jumping off the ship into the shallows with a big splash.

On the beach there was a big rock, just as the treasure map had promised.

Captain Diamond took six steps to the left. "One, two, three, four, five, six."

"Here we go!" she cried.

"Hooray!" cheered the pirates. They started to dig a hole with their shovels in the hot sun. Soon everyone was sweating. They dug and dug and dug—but there was no treasure.

"Oh dear," said Diamond.

"No treasure!" said Bosun Bob.

"Maybe it's a fake map," said Crewman Charlie.

They were all fed up. Then Billy looked at the map again. "Er, Captain," he said.

"What, Billy?" said Captain Diamond.

"I think the map might be upside down," said Billy.

Captain Diamond looked at the map again. "Do you know, Billy, I think you might be right!" she said.

Captain Diamond took six steps to the right. "One, two, three, four, five, six."

The pirates dug a new hole.

"Treasure!" they all cried.

"Thanks to Billy," said Captain Diamond. "And as a reward, Billy, you can have a dozen gold doubloons!"

Car Wash

David's dad was washing his car.

"I really hate this job!" he said to David and Josh. "If you want to earn some money, you should wash people's cars."

David and Josh thought this was a great idea. They made a big sign, filled some buckets with soapy water, and borrowed some sponges.

Soon afterward, Mr. Cole drove in. "Hello, boys," he said. "I'll be your first customer!"

David and Josh looked at the car. It was very muddy!

"This is going to take forever!" said David.

Melinda, who lived down the road, was walking by.

"Hello, Melinda!" David and Josh called.

"What are you doing?" asked Melinda. "That looks fun!"

David had an idea. "It is fun!" he lied. "If you give us $1, you can help."

"Thank you!" said Melinda, looking pleased. "I don't have the money, but I'll ask my dad for it later."

David handed Melinda a sponge and did a high five with Josh behind her back.

Melinda was a hard worker, and soon the car was sparkling.

"You've done a great job, boys!" said Mr. Cole. "Thank you."

Melinda's dad was the next person to pull into the driveway.

"Hello, Dad!" said Melinda. "Can we wash your car?"

David pointed to the sign. "It'll cost $1," he said. Melinda's dad got out his wallet.

"Please may I have $1 too, Dad?" asked Melinda. "I need to pay David and Josh for letting me help."

Her dad put the wallet back in his pocket. "You'll do nothing of the sort!" he replied, crossly.

He turned to David and Josh. "I'm going to speak to your parents!" he said.

David and Josh's parents were not happy! "You two can wash Melinda's dad's car for free," said Josh's mom.

"Then you can wash our car for free," added David's mom. David and Josh sighed.

"Can I help for free?" asked Melinda. "I love washing cars!"

Good-night Kiss

"It's bedtime now, Oakey," said Mom.

Oakey curled up in the chair. His ears began to droop and he muttered, "Oh, that's not fair!"

"Have a drink first," smiled Mom, "then you must go."

Oakey's ears drooped and off he went. But he was back in a flash!

"Where's your drink?" asked Mom. "You haven't been very long. You look scared, Oakey. Is there something wrong?"

"There's a ghost in the hallway, hovering about. Look, there it is floating just above the ground," he wailed.

"Oh, Oakey, you've made a mistake. That's no ghost. It's just an old coat, hanging on the hook!" laughed Mom.

Oakey's ears drooped and off he went. But he was back in a flash!

"Why aren't you in bed, Oakey?" asked Mom.

"There's a great big lump beneath the sheets. I'm scared it's going to pounce. Please come and see," sniffed Oakey.

"Oh, Oakey, you've made a mistake. The only thing

underneath the sheets is your old teddy bear," smiled Mom.

Oakey's ears drooped and he got into bed. But he didn't close his eyes.

"Why aren't you asleep?" asked Mom.

"There are huge creepy crawlies underneath my bed," complained Oakey.

"They're just your slippers, Oakey. They won't be creeping anywhere without your feet inside," grinned Mom.

"That's it now, Oakey. Time to say good-night." Mom turned and left the room, switching off the light.

Oakey lay in the dark for a little while. And then he saw it, standing by the door. The monster!

It moved across the floor and walked straight toward him.

The monster leaned over him and Oakey closed his eyes. What happened next gave Oakey an enormous surprise.

The monster picked him up and cuddled him tight. Monsters just don't do that. This couldn't be right!

Then Mom's voice whispered, "Don't worry, it's just me. When I said 'Good-night' just now, I forgot to give you this."

Then Monster Mom gave Oakey a good-night kiss!

King of the Castle

Ross and Alexis were exploring an old castle near the campsite they were staying on. They saw someone they knew.

"Oh no, it's Jaden," said Ross. Jaden was climbing a wall.

Alexis pointed to the big sign. It said DANGER.

"Come down!" said Alexis.

"You will fall!" said Ross. But Jaden carried on climbing. He stood on top of the wall. He marched up and down. "I'm the king of the castle!" he said.

"Look!" said Ross. "The wall is falling down."

"Jaden, you are in danger!" said Alexis.

DANGER

Bang! A few bricks fell off the top of the wall.

"Watch out, Jaden!" cried Alexis.

"Don't be such a scaredy-cat!" shouted Jaden, scornfully.

Crash! A whole section of the wall fell down. Jaden slipped...

"*Jaden!*" shouted Ross.

Jaden just managed to hold on to the top of the wall with his fingertips. "Help me!" he shouted. "Help me! I'm about to fall!"

"Hold on!" said Ross.

Ross and Alexis ran back to the campsite to get help.

Soon a fire engine arrived. The firefighters put a ladder against the wall and lifted Jaden down.

"Thank goodness you're safe," said Jaden's mom, giving him a big hug.

"Don't do that again," said a firefighter, sternly.

"I won't," said Jaden. "Thank you for saving me."

And for once it looked as though Jaden might mean it!

Witches on the Run

At night, when it's all dark and scary,
I peek from my covers, quite wary.
And there on the wall
Are shadows so tall—
Pointed hats, capes, and noses all hairy.

They love casting spells late at night,
Their cauldron glows with a strange light.
It bubbles and spits,
Spilling slimy green bits,
And gives me and Teddy a fright!

My mom says that I must be dreaming,
When I spy witches high on the ceiling.
But they keep me awake
With the noise that they make,
All that ear-piercing cackling and screaming!

But tonight when they come I'll be ready,
All I need is to keep my aim steady.
One squirt from my gun,
Will have them on the run,
Witches hate getting wet, don't they, Teddy?

Meet-on-the-Road

"Now, pray, where are you going?" said Meet-on-the-Road.
"To school sir, to school sir," said Child-as-it-Stood.
"What have you in your basket, child?" said Meet-on-the-Road.
"My dinner, sir, my dinner, sir," said Child-as-it-Stood.

"What have you for dinner, child?" said Meet-on-the-Road.
"Some pudding, sir, some pudding, sir," said Child-as-it-Stood.
"Oh then, I pray, give me a share," said Meet-on-the-Road.
"I've little enough for myself, sir," said Child-as-it-Stood.

"What have you got that cloak on for?" said Meet-on-the-Road.
"To keep the wind and cold from me," said Child-as-it-Stood.
"I wish the wind would blow through you," said Meet-on-the-Road.
"Oh, what a wish! What a wish!" said Child-as-it-Stood.

"Pray, what are those bells ringing for?" said Meet-on-the-Road.
"To ring bad spirits home again," said Child-as-it-Stood.
"Oh, then I must be going, child!" said Meet-on-the-Road.
"So fare you well, so fare you well," said Child-as-it-Stood.

Sports Day

It was Sports Day at school. First there was the running race. All the animals lined up.

"On your marks, get set, *Go!*" said Mrs. Beak, the teacher. Jake Giraffe had long legs. He won the running race.

Next was a beanbag race. Lucy Lion kept her head very still. She won the beanbag race.

Then there was a hopping race. Mikey Monkey won the hopping race.

But poor Helga Hippo didn't win a single race.

That playtime Helga sat on her own, feeling sorry for herself. "I'm no good at anything," she thought.

Then she heard loud shouts from the pond. Mikey had slipped in!

"Help!" he called. "I can't swim!"

"I can't swim, either!" said Jake.

"I can't swim either!" said Lucy.

"Help!" cried Mikey, desperately.

Helga could swim. She jumped in and saved Mikey. "I might not be a fast runner, a good beanbag balancer, or a great hopper," she said. "But I can swim!"

"Well done, Helga!" said Mrs. Beak.

A Stormy Day

"Lunchtime!"

It was time for the builders to eat. The builders went to their hut to drink coffee and eat sandwiches.

Digger had a rest. Dumper had a rest. Dozer had a rest.

Then a storm cloud came over. The wind began to blow and the rain began to fall.

"*Meow!*" mewed the cat who lived on the building site.

"The cat will get wet," said Digger.

"Her kittens will get cold," said Dumper. The cat was afraid. She hid her kittens in Digger's scoop.

"Look!" said the builders, when they came back from their lunch. The cat and her kittens were fast asleep curled up in Digger's scoop.

The builders took the cat and the kittens to the hut to keep them safe and dry from the storm.

Sippity, Sippity Sup

Sippity sup, sippity sup,
Bread and milk from a china cup.
Bread and milk from a bright silver spoon
Made of a piece of the bright silver moon.
Sippity sup, sippity sup,
Sippity, sippity sup.

Hannah Bantry

Hannah Bantry,
In the pantry,
Gnawing on a mutton bone;
How she gnawed it,
How she clawed it,
When she found herself alone.

Old King Cole

Old King Cole was a merry old soul,
And a merry old soul was he;
He called for his pipe, and he called for his bowl,
And he called for his fiddlers three.

Little Blue Ben

Little Blue Ben, who lives in the glen,
Keeps a blue cat and one blue hen,
Which lays of blue eggs a score and ten;
Where shall I find the little Blue Ben?

Eeper Weeper

Eeper Weeper, chimney sweeper,
Married a wife and could not keep her.
Married another,
Did not love her,
Up the chimney he did shove her!

Dame Trot

Dame Trot and her cat
Sat down for a chat;
The dame sat on this side
And puss sat on that.
"Puss," says the dame,
"Can you catch a rat,
Or a mouse in the dark?"
"Purr," says the cat.

The President's Secret

"I have to leave early today, Jed," said Mom, grabbing her keys. "See you later!"

As the front door slammed shut, Jed switched on the television. He didn't have to leave for school just yet.

He flicked onto the news channel. "No one knows what is wrong with the President," said a newscaster. "He hasn't been seen in public for over a week."

Jed yawned and then went into the study to get his bookbag. As he passed the computer, he couldn't resist checking to see what Mom was up to today. Jed's mom was a spy.

There was a photo of a bald man on the screen. He looked oddly familiar.

"The president's wig got lost last week," Jed read. He looked at the photo again and his eyes widened. The man in the photo was the president, without his thick mop of gray hair. The president wore a wig and no one knew!

Jed read on. "The president's

dog chewed up his spare
wig, and a new wig cannot
be made because the
president's wig-maker has
broken his arm in a skiing
accident. You must find
the lost wig as quickly as
possible, Agent Best."

Jed grinned. "I'll have to think of a good excuse for being
late for school today," he said.

Half an hour later, Jed was standing at the back of the
White House, where the president lived. He checked that
no one was looking and then quickly climbed the wall and
dropped into the garden. He sneaked up to the house, grinning
when he saw that the back door had a dog flap.

Jed squeezed through it and found himself in a large kitchen.

"Is that you, Bruno?" said a woman's voice. The voice was coming toward the kitchen.

Jed quickly ducked behind some recycling bins.

"Woof!" A big, shaggy dog brushed past him.

"Time for breakfast, Bruno," said the woman.

Jed saw a closet. "I'll wait in there while she feeds the dog," he thought, slipping inside.

It was a cleaning closet. As his eyes got used to the dark, Jed spotted something in the corner. "That's a strange mop," he thought.

He leaned down to take a closer look. It wasn't a mop at all.

"It's the missing wig!" Jed whispered. Someone had mistaken it for a mop head!

Jed shook the wig and coughed as a cloud of dust filled the closet.

When the kitchen was empty again, Jed crept out of the closet, clutching the wig.

He went off to find the Oval Office. When he found the right door, Jed hung the scruffy wig onto the door handle.

Then Jed gave the door two short knocks and hid behind a nearby chair.

The door opened. Jed heard a gasp—and then saw a hand snatch up the wig and slam the door shut again.

Jed smiled. "I guess it's time for school now," he said to himself.

That evening, Mom arrived home from work early, in a very good mood.

Jed was watching the news. "Look at the president!" he said. "He sure is having a bad hair day!"

One, Two

One, two, whatever you do,
Start it well and carry it through.
Try, try, never say die,
Things will come right,
You know, by and by.

Old Bandy Legs

As I was going to sell my eggs,
I met a man with bandy legs;
Bandy legs and crooked toes,
I tripped up his heels and he fell on his nose.

I Do Not Like Thee

I do not like thee, Doctor Fell,
The reason why, I cannot tell;
But this I know, and know full well,
I do not like thee, Doctor Fell.

My Mommy's Maid

Dingty diddlety,
My mommy's maid,
She stole oranges,
I am afraid;
Some in her pocket,
Some in her sleeve,
She stole oranges,
I do believe.

Charlie Wag

Charlie Wag,
Charlie Wag,
Ate the pudding
And left the bag.

Sunshine

A sunshiny shower
Won't last half an hour.

Farmyard Chase

Mother Hen sat on her nest and shook out her soft, fluffy feathers. She had an egg to keep warm. She had been sitting there for hours.

"I'm hungry," thought Mother Hen. Suddenly, Mother Hen saw a patch of sunlight by the barn door. She had an idea. She rolled her egg carefully over into the sun and packed some hay around it. "That will keep you warm," she said to her egg. "I won't be long."

And off she went to find some corn.

Horse came trotting up to the barn. He was hungry, too. He saw the hay by the barn door.

"Yummy!" he neighed, as he pushed his smooth, velvety muzzle into the hay. Bump! Horse's nose nudged Mother Hen's egg.

The egg rocked, and then it rolled. It rolled across the yard.

"Oh no!" neighed Horse. He trotted after the egg as it tumbled toward a pile of apples under the apple tree.

Pig was snuffling around the apple tree as the egg rolled past his nose.

"Oh no!" squealed Pig. "Catch that egg before it cracks!" And he scampered after the egg as it tumbled into the grassy meadow.

Sheep was munching the tufty grass in the meadow as the egg rolled past her.

"Oh no!" bleated Sheep. "Catch that egg before it cracks!" And she skipped after the egg as it tumbled down the hill.

At the bottom of the hill, Cow was lying down, having a rest after lunch. Bump! The egg bounced against Cow's nose.

"Ouch!" mooed Cow. "What was that?" And she stared at the egg. Horse, Pig, and Sheep came running down the hill.

"Catch that egg before it cracks!" they called.

"I have caught it," replied Cow.

"My egg!" clucked Hen, flapping her way down the hill.

Just then, there was a loud *Crack!*

"Someone must have cracked it!" clucked Hen. *Crack!* The crack got bigger still.

Suddenly, the egg cracked wide open. Out hopped a soft, fluffy ball of yellow feathers.

"It was me!" cheeped the little fluffy chick. "I cracked it all by myself!"

Fire! Fire!

"Get out of the way!" the sirens say,
The big red fire engine is on its way.

Around the corner with a screech of tires,
The fire engine races to put out fires.

Listen to the sirens! They seem to say,
"Coming through! Please make way!"

See the smoke! The barn fire grows!
Quickly! Quickly! Roll out the hose.

Here comes the water—*swoosh!*—from the spout.
Splish! Splash! Hiss! And the fire is out!

Choo! Choo!

All aboard, off we go!
The wheels are turning—start off slow!

Choo! Choo! Choo! Count with me,
Shiny carriages, one, two, three.

Up the hill, along the track,
Faster, faster, clickety-clack!

Across the bridge the train goes by,
Clouds of smoke puff way up high.

Here's the tunnel… *Whoo! Whoo!*
The whistle blows. We're coming through!

Chuffa! Chuffa! At last we're here!
"Hip hooray!" the passengers cheer.

The Fantastic Firework

Whoosh! A fountain of gold stars fell through the night sky. It was Fourth of July in the town of Fulshear and a big crowd had gathered to enjoy the spectacular fireworks display.

High above them, Ag the Alien was coming in to land in his brand-new supercharged spaceship.

"Ah, home again!" he said. Unfortunately, Ag wasn't anywhere near his home. He didn't know it, but he was completely lost.

Down below, a boy named Mike tugged at his father's arm. "Hey! Look over there, Dad," he cried. "That rocket's coming down, not going up!"

Ag thought he had made a perfect landing. Then he looked through his sky screen and gasped. He hastily pressed the *Where Am I?* switch, and a message flashed up: *Planet Earth.*

"Earth!" shrieked Ag. He realized that he must have activated the hyperthrust device by mistake and that he'd better press it again, quick, when something happened that stopped him in his tracks.

Two fountains blossomed across the sky in a brilliant flash of yellow.

Now, Ag loved fireworks. In fact, everyone did on his planet.

"Just think how thrilled everyone at home would be," Ag thought, "if I let off a new firework they'd never seen before." So Ag armed himself with a laser megablaster, jumped out of the spacecraft, and hurried off toward the Fulshear fireworks show.

Bang! He ran straight into Mike, who had come to check out the strange rocket.

"Aagh!" yelled Mike.

"Pleased to meet you," said Ag, feeling very confused. He had been about to blow the odd-looking creature to smithereens. But it had known his name!

Looking at the megablaster, Mike quickly decided it would be wise to make friends, if that was what the alien wanted to do. "Er, pleased to meet you, too," he replied.

"Now," said Ag. "I need your fireworks."

"I know just what you want," said Mike, thinking quickly. "It's over there in that clump of trees, and it's the best thing in the show. But you'll need to beam it up, because it's so big."

Ag was delighted. He beamed the giant firework aboard and whooshed away, seconds before everyone started to gather for the grand finale. To Mike's surprise, they started clapping, as if the grand finale had already happened.

"What a fantastic firework!" Mike's dad said. "It looked just like a huge space rocket being launched!" Mike grinned to himself.

And meanwhile, on the other side of the galaxy, the letters of Fulshear ignited in a blaze of golden fountains.

"Where did you get it?" Ag's friends exclaimed.

"Oh, just a little place I know," he grinned.

Monster Munch

I may be big and hairy
And I may look mean and tough,
But I'm a nice, kind monster,
And I've simply had enough!

It's really most distressing
When you scream and run away—
I have no plans to eat you,
All I want to do is play!

Oh, can't you see I'm lonely?
Can't you tell I'm feeling blue?
I've got no friends to talk to,
But I like the look of you!

I'm just about to make some lunch,
And I'd love it if you'd come.
You will? Oh, great, that's perfect!
Ha, ha—I tricked you! Yum!

London Bridge

London Bridge is falling down,
Falling down, falling down.
London Bridge is falling down,
My fair lady.

Build it up with iron bars,
Iron bars, iron bars,
Build it up with iron bars,
My fair lady.

Iron bars will bend and break,
Bend and break, bend and break,
Iron bars will bend and break,
My fair lady.

Build it up with stone so strong,
Stone so strong, stone so strong,
Huzza! 'twill last for ages long,
My fair lady.

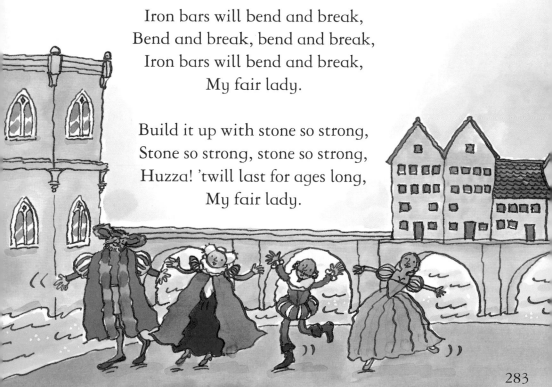

Little Elephant's Clever Trick

Little Elephant set off for a walk. Today he wanted to explore. He hadn't gone far when he met Zebra.

Little Elephant had never seen a zebra before. He looked at Zebra's snazzy stripes. Then he looked at his own plain skin. Little Elephant was puzzled.

"Excuse me," Little Elephant said. "Why are you stripy?"

"So I can hide," replied Zebra. "When I'm in the grass, out on the plain, it's really hard to see me. I'll show you!"

He galloped off. Little Elephant tried to see where he went, but Zebra had disappeared.

Little Elephant was amazed. "You're right! It is hard to see you. That's so clever."

Little Elephant wandered on. Before long, Little Elephant met Giraffe. He had never seen a giraffe before.

Little Elephant looked at Giraffe's pretty patches. Then he looked at his own gray skin.

"Excuse me," Little Elephant said. "Why are you covered in patches?"

"So I can hide," Giraffe replied. "When I'm under the trees and the sun's shining, it's really hard to see me. I'll show you!"

Giraffe walked over to some trees. Little Elephant tried to see where she went, but Giraffe had disappeared. Little Elephant was impressed.

"You're right! It is hard to see you. That's so clever." And Little Elephant wandered on.

Little Elephant was starting to feel very sad. "I can't hide anywhere," he thought. "Everyone would be able to see me. I wish I was like Zebra or Giraffe."

He knelt down, bowed his head, and began to cry.

Giraffe and Zebra came back with Crocodile. "Where's Little Elephant?" asked Giraffe. "He was here a minute ago."

"Well, he's not here now," said Zebra. "There's just that old rock over there."

The rock began to giggle. "It's me!" called Little Elephant. "I'm not a rock!"

"What a clever trick!" smiled Zebra.

"You don't need grass or trees," laughed Giraffe.

"You can hide anywhere, just like that," added Zebra.

"So I can," said Little Elephant.

"We came to see if you'd like to play," said Little Elephant's new friends.

"Yes, please!" replied Little Elephant. "I'd like to play hide-and-seek."

The Grand Old Duke of York

The grand old Duke of York,
He had ten thousand men;
He marched them up to the top of the hill,
And he marched them down again!

And when they were up they were up,
And when they were down they were down;
And when they were only halfway up,
They were neither up nor down.

What Is the Rhyme for Porringer?

What is the rhyme for porringer?
The King he had a daughter fair,
And gave the Prince of Orange her.

Go to Bed

Go to bed late,
Stay very small;
Go to bed early
Grow very tall.

Gray Goose and Gander

Gray goose and gander,
Waft your wings together,
And carry the good king's daughter
Over the one strand river.

Ten Little Men

Ten little men standing straight,
Ten little men open the gate,
Ten little men all in a ring,
Ten little men bow to the king,
Ten little men dance all day,
Ten little men hide away.

I Met a Man

As I was going up the stair
I met a man who wasn't there.
He wasn't there again today—
Oh how I wish he'd go away!

Tickly Sheep

One morning, Farmer Fred was in the kitchen having his hair cut. Farmer Fred's wife Jenny was snipping away with the scissors.

"Hurry up," said Farmer Fred. "I've got to shear all the sheep today."

"Well, stop wriggling," laughed Jenny.

"But it tickles," chuckled Farmer Fred.

"I've never known anyone make such a fuss about having their hair cut," laughed Jenny, making the final snip.

Farmer Fred and Patch went up to Fern Hill to round up the sheep. Farmer Fred whistled a signal to Patch: *Peep! Peeeep!* Patch ran around the field, herding the sheep toward the yard.

Farmer Fred whistled a different signal: *Peeeep! Peep!* Patch soon had the sheep lined up outside the barn.

Inside the barn, Farmer Fred switched on his shears. *Whiz, whiz, whiz* went the shears.

"There's nothing quite like shearing sheep," he smiled, and began to sing.

One by one, Farmer Fred sheared the sheep. The woolly fleeces that came off the sheep collected on the barn floor. All went well until it was Shirley Sheep's turn.

Whiz, whiz, went the shears. As soon as the buzzing shears touched her side, Shirley began to wriggle and jiggle.

"Stop wriggling," cried Farmer Fred, as he tried to hold her still. He had forgotten just how ticklish Shirley was!

"Rumbling radishes!" Fred gasped, when he had finished. Shirley had wriggled around so much that she had big bald patches all over her woolly fleece. She looked very peculiar!

"Never fear, I've got an idea!" cried Farmer Fred cheerfully. He dashed off to his workshop and disappeared inside.

Very soon, Farmer Fred came out of the workshop, holding two old tires tied onto some rope.

"This," Farmer Fred said grandly, "is my Super Sheep-defleecer!"

Farmer Fred helped Shirley Sheep to step through the tires and slowly lifted her off the ground. He turned on the shears and tried again.

And although Shirley wriggled and giggled, Farmer Fred sheared off all her wool.

Farmer Fred let Shirley Sheep down and helped her from the tires.

"Baa?" asked Shirley Sheep. She looked at the other animals. But they were all laughing so much at Shirley Sheep's stripy haircut they couldn't answer.

While Fred collected up the sheep fleeces, the animals gathered around Shirley Sheep.

"She can't possibly go around looking like that," said Hetty Hen. "Everyone will laugh at her."

"We have to do something," agreed Harry Horse. "Patch, what can we do?"

Suddenly Patch remembered Farmer Fred having his hair cut.

"Woof, woof!" he barked. "Leave it to me." Patch raced to the kitchen where Jenny had put the scissors, comb, and mirror into a bowl.

"Woof, woof!" barked Patch, pushing the bowl outside just as Farmer Fred was crossing the yard.

"What's that, Patch?" laughed Fred. "I don't have time to give you a haircut now." Just then Shirley trotted up.

"Hold on!" said Farmer Fred. "I've had an even better idea!" He picked up the bowl and raced back to the barn.

Before long Shirley was sitting in her very own wool-cutting parlor.

"Now, would madam like a short and curly cut?" laughed Farmer Fred, as he began snipping away.

And this time, Shirley didn't giggle or wriggle until all that was left were curly bangs.

"Perfect," said Farmer Fred, as he tied a huge blue ribbon in Shirley's lovely curls.

Shirley walked proudly around the farmyard. Everyone, including Jenny, gathered around to admire her.

They all agreed that she was the prettiest sheep on the farm.

"I've never known anyone make such a fuss about having their hair cut," said Farmer Fred. Jenny looked at Patch and laughed.

Yard Makeover

Josh's mom was doing some gardening. It gave Josh an idea.

He hurried around to David's. "Let's see if anyone will pay us to do some gardening," he suggested.

Mr. Peacock across the road was happy to be asked. "I'll pay you to mow the grass and do some weeding," he said. "The lawn mower is in the shed."

"My turn first!" said David, starting up the engine.

It wasn't easy to steer the mower in a straight line. "Oops!" David muttered, as he plowed through a flowerbed.

Josh began to pull up weeds. "Oops!" he said, as each weed turned out to be a carrot.

Mr. Peacock came hurrying down the walkway. "My beautiful flowers!" he cried. "And my prize carrots!"

"We're sorry, Mr. Peacock," said Josh.

"We're not very good at gardening," David added.

With a sigh, Mr. Peacock bent down to inspect the damage

to his carrots. He picked up something shiny from the earth.

"What's this?" he asked. And then he gasped. "It's a Roman coin!" he said. "Quick boys, get digging—see if you can find any more!"

Together, Josh, David, and Mr. Peacock dug up a whole mound of Roman coins. "My mom runs the store at the local museum," said David. "She says that the curator there knows all there is to know about the Romans."

"Let's take them down there!" said Mr. Peacock.

The museum curator was very excited when she saw the coins. "These are very rare!" she said. "They might prove that there were once Romans living around here."

She looked at Mr. Peacock. "And they're probably very valuable!"

Back home, Mr. Peacock paid Josh and David.

"I think you've given us too much money, Mr. Peacock," said David.

"No I haven't," he said. "It's to say thank you for helping me find the coins." Then he winked at them. "Now I'll be able to afford a proper gardener!"

Doing Dishes

When I was a little boy
I washed my mommy's dishes;
I put my finger in one eye,
And pulled out golden fishes.

What's the News?

"What's the news of the day,
Good neighbor, I pray?"
"They say the balloon
Is gone up to the moon."

The Queen of Hearts

The Queen of Hearts, she made some tarts,
All on a summer's day;
The Knave of Hearts, he stole the tarts,
And took them clean away.
The King of Hearts called for the tarts,
And beat the Knave full sore;
The Knave of Hearts brought back the tarts,
And vowed he'd steal no more.

King Arthur

When famed King Arthur ruled this land
He was a goodly king:
He took three pecks of barley meal
To make a bag pudding.
A rare pudding the king did make,
And stuffed it well with plums;
And in it put such lumps of fat,
As big as my two thumbs.
The king and queen did eat thereof,
And noblemen beside,
And what they could not eat that night
The queen next morning fried.

Cobbler, Cobbler

Cobbler, cobbler, mend my shoe,
Get it done by half past two;
Stitch it up, and stitch it down,
Then I'll give you half a crown.

Rain Before Seven

Rain before seven,
Fine by eleven.

Two Heads Are Worse Than One

Clay and Rye were fed up with their parents always giving them chores to do—so, one evening, they decided to run away.

The boys hadn't gone far when they realized that they'd accidentally wandered into Monster Forest. And not only were they lost, but there was something large and heavy coming toward them.

The boys shrank back in fright. A huge monster appeared, green and warty, like a giant toad. It had two heads. One looked kind and friendly, but the other looked bad tempered.

"Oh, hello," said the friendly head when it saw them. "Company at last. It's very nice to see you…"

"That's enough small talk," growled the ugly head. "I'm going to eat them."

Rye buried his head in his brother's coat.

"We can't eat them, Bad Head. They're far too skinny. Nothing but skin and bone." And the nice head winked at the two boys, as if to say, "Don't worry. I'll look after you."

"Um," agreed Bad Head. "We'll keep them prisoners. Fatten them up a bit, and then eat them."

They all spent a busy day in the forest looking for food, and when evening fell, they sat beside a warm fire and talked. Good Head said that having to feed a few chickens now and again wasn't such a bad thing if you had a warm house to live in and a soft bed, and the boys had to agree that the life they'd run away from wasn't so bad after all.

"What nonsense," grumbled Bad Head, rather sleepily.

Good Head winked at the boys. Bad Head was lolling forward, yawning. Soon he was fast asleep and snoring loudly.

"Quickly," whispered Good Head. They hurried as fast and as quietly as they could out of the forest.

"Thank you," whispered the boys to Good Head.

"My pleasure," said Good Head. "Now hurry."

Clay and Rye scampered across the open fields toward home as fast as they could.

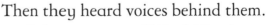

Then they heard voices behind them.

"They got away!" Bad Head was shouting. "You useless monster. Why didn't you stop them?"

The voices faded into the forest and the boys ran home. And they never ventured into Monster Forest, or complained about their chores, ever again!

I Just Can't Sleep

It's time to sleep.
I've brushed my teeth,
And read my book,
I've put my bathrobe
On the hook, and...
I just can't sleep.
The bed's too hot,
The light's too bright,
There are far too many
Sounds tonight, and...
Maybe I'll sleep.
I think I might,
I think I'll—yawn –
Turn out the light.
Good night.
Zzzzzz...

Vacation Time

We're off on vacation. Oh, what fun!
There may be rain or there may be sun.
But we'll all have a lovely time together,
And enjoy ourselves, whatever the weather!

Bunny in a Hurry

Tick tock! It's eight o'clock!
Can you tell the time?
Wake up, Bunny! Don't be late!
It's time to rise and shine.

Tick tock! It's twelve o'clock!
No time for any stops!
Bunny has a bouncy lunch,
Munching as he hops!

Tick tock! It's three o'clock!
So many things to do,
Like finding everything he needs
To make a carrot stew.

Tick tock! It's six o'clock!
And something smells delicious!
Hurry, Bunny, eat your stew!
You've got to wash the dishes!

Tick tock! It's seven o'clock!
Shhhh! Don't make a peep.
What a busy day it's been.
Now Bunny's fast asleep!

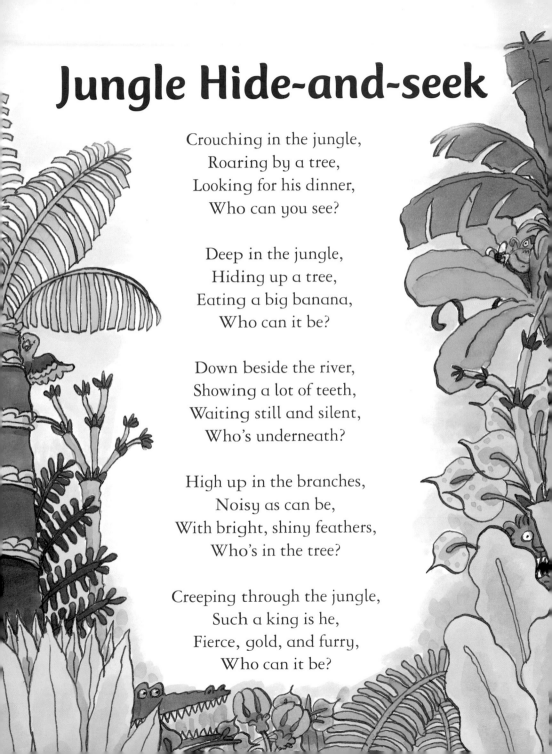

Jungle Hide-and-seek

Crouching in the jungle,
Roaring by a tree,
Looking for his dinner,
Who can you see?

Deep in the jungle,
Hiding up a tree,
Eating a big banana,
Who can it be?

Down beside the river,
Showing a lot of teeth,
Waiting still and silent,
Who's underneath?

High up in the branches,
Noisy as can be,
With bright, shiny feathers,
Who's in the tree?

Creeping through the jungle,
Such a king is he,
Fierce, gold, and furry,
Who can it be?

The Mountain Mission

Jed was helping Elise the babysitter prepare dinner when Mom arrived home. She came into the kitchen, and put two plane tickets onto the table.

"Surprise! We're flying to Switzerland first thing tomorrow," she said. "So we'd better start packing!"

"Are we going skiing?" asked Jed excitedly.

"Yes, we're staying in a luxury ski resort," replied Mom.

"Wow!" said Elise. "I wish I were coming!"

Jed was curious. Why had his mom suddenly decided to take this vacation? It must have something to do with her work as a spy, he guessed.

While Mom was packing, Jed sneaked upstairs, turned on her computer, and checked her e-mails.

He soon found out why they were really going. Some plans for a new spy plane had been stolen and Mom's mission was to get them back. An enemy agent called Max Blatt had the plans in his Swiss mountain hideout.

"This could be

Mom's most dangerous mission yet," Jed said to himself. "Good job I'm going along, too."

"Wow!" said Jed, as they arrived in the ski resort. He almost forgot why they were really there as he looked up at the snow-covered mountains. He couldn't wait to get out on those ski runs. He loved skiing.

Mom was looking up, too. Jed followed her gaze. She was staring at a building at the top of a nearby mountain.

"That must be Blatt's hideout," Jed guessed. It was a long way up. Jed knew that his mom wasn't very good at skiing. She'd never make it all the way down that mountain. "I must act fast, before Mom tries anything stupid," he said to himself.

While Mom was unpacking, Jed went to explore the resort. Finding a store that sold party costumes, he had an idea. He took out the savings he'd brought with him, paid for a St. Bernard dog costume, and then smuggled it into his room.

"At least this silly disguise will keep me warm in the snow!" Jed thought as he put on the furry outfit the following morning.

There was only one way up the mountain, in the ski lift. Some skiers laughed when Jed got in.

"I didn't know dogs could ski!" one of them joked. At the top

of the mountain, Jed left the skiers behind. He made his way to the security fence surrounding Blatt's hideout and climbed over it.

Sneaking in through an open window, Jed found Blatt's office and began to look around for the plans. "They must be in here somewhere," he thought.

Suddenly, three large dogs appeared. Jed was about to run when he saw that they didn't look at all fierce. They wanted to make friends.

"My costume must have fooled them," Jed thought with a relieved grin.

He found the plans, grabbed them, and ran to the back door, almost tripping over a dog basket. "That will come in handy!" he said, picking it up. It was great fun sledding

down the mountain in the basket.

Soon Jed was back in his hotel. He went up to the reception desk.

"Will you send these papers up to Frances Best in Room 303, please?" he asked, handing over the plans.

"Mom will love the room service in this hotel!" Jed chuckled to himself.

My Hobby Horse

I had a little hobby horse, it was well shod,
It carried me to London, niddety nod,
And when we got to London we heard a great shout,
Down fell my hobby horse and I cried out:
"Up again, hobby horse, if thou be a beast,
When we get to our town we will have a feast,
And if there be but a little, why thou shall have some,
And dance to the bagpipes and beating of the drum."

Engine, Engine

Engine, engine, number nine,
Sliding down Chicago line;
When she's polished she will shine,
Engine, engine, number nine.

Red Sky

Red sky at night,
Shepherd's delight;
Red sky in the morning,
Shepherd's warning.

Robin Hood

Robin Hood has gone to the wood;
He'll come back again if we are good.

There Was a Little Boy

There was a little boy and a little girl
Lived in an alley;
Says the little boy to the little girl,
"Shall I, oh, shall I?"
Says the little girl to the little boy,
"What shall we do?"
Says the little boy to the little girl,
"I will kiss you."

And That's All

There was an old man,
And he had a calf,
And that's half;
He took him out of the stall,
And put him on the wall,
And that's all.

Lost and Found

It was Show and Tell time in Joe's class.

Sam and Jack showed their new Perry Hill soccer shirts.

"Who else is a Perry Hill fan?" asked Miss Bell.

Joe put up his hand. So did Clare, the new girl in class.

Joe sighed. He really wanted to go and see Perry Hill play that Saturday, but it cost five dollars and he didn't have any pocket money left.

During recess, Joe was kicking a ball around on his own when he saw something fluttering by. Joe leaped and grabbed it. It was a five dollar bill. He put the money in his pocket. Score!

After break, though, Clare was very upset.

"I've lost five dollars," she said to Miss Bell.

Joe thought about it.

He knew that the money was Clare's. Deep down, he had known all along that it wasn't his.

"I found it," said Joe.

"Thank you!" said Clare.

"Well done, Joe!" said Miss Bell.

The next day after school, Joe saw

Jared Jones at the school gate. He was the top forward at Perry Hill soccer club.

"Look!" said Joe to Sam and Jack. "Jared Jones! I wonder what he's doing here?"

"He's talking to Clare!" said Sam.

"Why isn't he talking to us?" said Jack. "We're much better at soccer than she is."

Then Clare called across the playground, "Over here, Joe!"

Joe went across the playground toward Jared. He felt a bit nervous about meeting him. Jared was such an amazing soccer player! Joe really hoped that one day he would be as good as Jared was.

"Jared is my big brother," Clare told Joe.

"Wow!" said Joe.

"Thanks for helping my sister," said Jared, handing Joe a ticket. Joe looked. It was three tickets to Saturday's match, in the best seats in the whole stadium.

"See you at the game on Saturday," said Jared. "And I hope you and your friends can come and meet the rest of the Perry Hill team after the game as well."

"Thanks!" said Joe.

Vicky, the Very Silly Vet

"Good morning!" called Vet Vicky as she opened the door to her office. "How are all my animals today?"

She lined up the breakfast bowls and animal feed on the table and began to put out the food. Then... *Ding!* went the doorbell.

"Oh!" cried Vicky. "My first patient is here already!" As quickly as she could, she put the bowls in the cages—but didn't look to see who was getting what! Patch the puppy got the bird seed, Hickory and Dickory the mice got the dog food, Percy the Parrot got the cat food, and Tabby got the mice's sunflower seeds! What's more, Vicky had left all the cage doors wide open.

Fortunately, this had happened before and the animals knew just what to do. Hickory and Dickory found their sunflower seeds in Tabby's basket, Tabby discovered her cat food in Percy's cage, Percy pecked at his bird seed in Patch's cage, and Patch found his dog food in the mouse cage.

"Come in," said Vicky to her first patient. Then a thought crossed her mind. Hadn't she left the cage doors open? She gulped. What dreadful mess would there be?

But the clever animals were all back in their own cages. Vicky saw the clean and tidy room and grinned. "Treats for dinner!" she whispered.

Foolish Builder Benny

One morning, Benny the builder arrived at Mary the mailwoman's house.

"I want you to build a playhouse for my grandchildren," she said. "It should have two doors, five windows, and a sloping roof."

Mary left for the post office, and Benny went out to start work. He tried to remember everything that Mary had said, but he got confused. Was it five windows and two doors? Or two windows and five doors? Was the roof flat or sloping? Benny decided he would just have to do the best he could.

When Mary got home from work what a surprise she had! The playhouse's roof was flat. There were five doors on one side of the house, and two windows on another side.

"It's all wrong!" said Mary. "How will you fix it in time?"

Benny didn't have a chance to answer, because just then Mary's five grandchildren arrived.

"Look! A playhouse!" they cried. "There's a door for each of us! And we can climb on the roof! Thank you, Grandma!"

"Well, I think you should thank Benny," said Mary, smiling.

Benny smiled too. "I just did my best," he said.

Fearless Firefighter Fred

Fred hurried into the fire station with a bag of nice plump hot dogs. It was his turn to cook lunch for the firemen on the shift.

"Ooops!" he said, as he bumped into Benny the builder, who had come to repair the door.

Suddenly the alarm bell rang.

"Emergency!" cried the firemen, sliding down the pole and into their firefighting gear.

"What about the hot dogs?" cried Fred.

"I'll look after them for you!" called Benny.

The emergency was in Tony's Pizza Parlor—one of the pizza ovens had caught fire!

"We'll have that blaze out in a jiffy," said Fred.

"Thank you!" said Tony, as the firefighters took their equipment back to the truck. "I can get back to baking pizzas now!"

"Look!" said Fred. "Smoke up ahead!"

The siren wailed as the engine raced to the scene of the fire. The smoke was coming from the fire station!

"Sorry, fellows," said Benny, running out. "I burned the hot dogs."

Fortunately, Fred had an idea.

"Don't worry, guys," he said. "A yummy extra-large pizza will be a perfect lunch for all of us!"

Marvelous Mary Mailwoman

"Good morning, Mary!" said Mr. Price the postmaster. "Your mailbag is all ready. It looks full today!"

Mary rushed around the corner of Jackson Road on her bicycle. But her bike started to get slower and slower. She had a flat tire.

"Oh no!" said Mary. "I'll have to walk my round today!"

Mary rushed and hurried, but by eleven o'clock her mailbag was still half full. Then suddenly she saw something that gave her a great idea.

"Jack, may I borrow your skateboard, please?" Mary asked.

Mary had never been on a skateboard before. She wibbled and wobbled... then *whooshed* down the street.

Mary finished her round at lightning speed. "This is quicker than walking," she said, "and much more fun than my bike!"

"Well done, Mary!" said Mr. Price, when Mary got back to the post office. "Benny the builder brought back your bike. We'll have to fix that flat right away."

"Oh, there's no hurry, Mr. Price," said Mary. "I've found a better form of transportation for a marvelous mailwoman!"

The Queen's Dessert

Martin was the youngest, smallest, and most hard-worked kitchen boy in the kitchens of the Queen of Hungerbert.

People shouted at him all day long: "Take this to the Queen!" "The Princess needs this now!" "Quickly!" "Move!"

One day the cook shouted at Martin, as usual.

"Take this dessert to the Queen! Now!" she said, giving Martin a dish of bananas and custard.

Martin took it to the Queen. The Queen took a bite.

"I like banana," she said. "But I don't like custard."

Martin went back to the kitchen.

Cook made gelatin and ice cream. Martin took it to the Queen.

The Queen took a bite. "I like ice cream," she said. "But I don't like the gelatin."

Cook made apple pie and cream.

"I like cream," said the Queen. "But I don't like pie."

"Oh dear!" said Cook. "The Queen only likes banana, ice cream, and cream."

"That makes a banana split!" said Martin.

"You might just be right, Martin," said Cook. She made a banana split.

Martin took it to the Queen. She took a bite.

"I love it!" she said.

Martin went back to the kitchen and told Cook.

"Well done, Martin!" said Cook.

Mikey Is Busy

It was quiet time at school. All the animals were busy. All except Mikey Monkey. Mikey didn't like quiet time. He liked noisy-running-around-and-swinging-from-trees time.

Lucy Lion was deep in a book. Mikey tiptoed up and closed the covers with a snap.

"Go away, Mikey," said Lucy. "You've made me lose my place!"

Helga Hippo was painting a picture of some flowers. Mikey tipped over the paint. Red paint went all over the floor.

"Mikey!" said Helga.

Jake was building a block tower. It was almost twenty bricks high! Then Mikey deliberately bumped into the blocks...

"Mikey!" cried Jake. "That was my tallest tower ever."

Then Mikey stood on one of the school chairs. He balanced on one foot, then on the other foot. He leaned backward...

Crash! The chair fell over onto the ground.

Mrs. Beak the teacher looked up from her desk.

"Are you busy, Mikey?" she said.

"No," said Mikey.

"This mess you've made will keep you busy then, Mikey!" said Mrs. Beak. "Tidy up!"

For Sale

Joseph and Olivia got out of the moving van and looked at their new house. The "For Sale" sign was still up outside it.

"I don't like it," said Olivia.

"Our old house was much better," said Joseph.

Mom and Dad didn't say anything, but Olivia and Joseph could tell that they were thinking the same thing.

Inside, all the rooms were empty. The sound of the family's footsteps echoed.

"It doesn't feel like home," said Joseph. Then he heard a noise from the next room.

"*Meow! Meow! Meow!*"

Joseph ran next door. In a corner of the room was a cat and her three kittens.

"Look, Mom!" cried Joseph.

"She must have sneaked in while the house was empty," said Mom. "We can't throw them out. It was their home before it was ours!"

Olivia stroked the cat. Joseph gently stroked one of the kittens.

"Now it feels like home," Joseph said.

Fancy Flying

Penelope Parrot and her mom, Portia, were having a wonderful afternoon watching the Fancy Flying Display Team. Penelope could hardly believe her eyes, as she saw the birds swoop and speed through the sky, doing their amazing tricks and wonderful stunts.

"I want to be just like them," thought Penelope.

Penelope had only learned to fly a short time ago—so she didn't really know how fast or how far she could go.

"I think you need some expert training if you want to be a Fancy Flyer," said Mom.

"But I don't know any experts," said Penelope.

"I know an expert," said Mom. "My uncle Percy has just arrived for a visit. He was a member of the original Fancy Flying team!"

So Percy and Penelope practiced and practiced, but Penelope couldn't stop spinning and crashing and falling.

"Well Penelope, are you ready to be a Fancy Flyer?" Mom asked, when she got home.

"Oh yes," said Penelope. "And I know just what my specialty will be... watching from the audience!"

Hippo's Vacation

It was a warm, sunny morning in the jungle.

"A perfect time for a nice, long, relaxing vacation," thought Howard Hippo. "And there's nothing a hippo loves more than wallowing."

Wallowing in the river was Howard's favorite thing to do. He found a nice, cool, muddy spot and settled in. Howard had decided that on this vacation, he would wallow all the way to Hippo Hollow, a famous hippo vacation location. He was very excited about meeting new hippo friends there.

After three days of floating downstream, Howard arrived at Hippo Hollow. "It's even more beautiful than I imagined!" he exclaimed.

The next few days were the best of Howard's life. He had mud baths, made new hippo friends, and splashed around in the cold water showers.

"I can't believe I haven't been on vacation here before," thought Howard.

And from that moment on, Howard went to Hippo Hollow on his vacation every year!

Stop That Thief!

Ross and Alexis were at the amusement park near their vacation campsite.

"What should we go on first?" said Alexis.

"The Ferris Wheel!" said Ross. They climbed into the swinging chairs and carefully fastened their safety belts.

And they were off! The wheel turned. Ross and Alexis rose up... up... up... into the air. They could see all the park.

"There's Jayden and Kim!" said Alexis. Jayden and Kim, who were staying in the tent next to them, were at the coconut stall.

The wheel went around and around. Then it started to slow down. The ride was nearly over.

Then Ross grabbed Alexis's arm. "Look down there!" he said. A man was stealing a purse!

"Stop that thief!" they shouted.

As soon as the Ferris Wheel stopped, Alexis and Ross jumped off.

"Look, there he is!" said Alexis.

"Stop that thief!"

shouted Ross, sprinting after him.

They chased the thief past the cotton candy stall, past the Helter-skelter, past Brianna's Bumper Cars, and past the Marvelous Merry-go-round.

"Ouch!" said a man, as Ross bumped right into him.

"Sorry!" gasped Ross.

The thief ran past the coconut stall towards the exit.

"Jayden!" called Ross. "Stop that thief!"

Four coconuts rolled out in front of the thief. His legs slid out from under him.

"Aaaargh!" He fell to the ground.

"That stopped you!" said Jayden.

"Well done, Jayden!" said Alexis.

The thief was led away by the police. "You've got some questions to answer, young man," the policeman said.

"Thank you!" said the purse's owner.

"You can all have free rides for the day," said the amusement park owner. "Anything you like. And you can have as much free food as you can eat."

"Great!" said the four friends, smiling.

Warning

The robin and the redbreast,
The robin and the wren:
If you take them from their nest
You'll never thrive again.

The Little, Rusty, Dusty Miller

Oh, the little, rusty, dusty miller,
Dusty was his coat,
Dusty was his color,
Dusty was the kiss
I got from the miller.
If I had my pockets
Full of gold and silver,
I would give it all
To my dusty miller.

Mr. East's Feast

Mr. East gave a feast;
Mr. North laid the cloth;
Mr. West did his best;
Mr. South burned his mouth
With eating a hot potato.

Catch Him

Catch him, crow! Carry him, kite!
Take him away till the apples are ripe;
When they are ripe and ready to fall,
Here comes a baby, apples and all.

Wine and Cakes

Wine and cakes for gentlemen,
Hay and corn for horses,
A cup of ale for good old wives,
And kisses for the lasses.

Wee Willie Winkie

Wee Willie Winkie runs through the town,
Upstairs and downstairs in his nightgown,
Peeping through the keyhole, crying through the lock,
"Are the children in their beds? It's past eight o'clock!"

Try It, You'll Like It!

It was the last day of school before the winter vacation and Sophia and Daniel were really excited.

"We're taking snowboarding lessons over the vacation," Sophia told all their classmates.

"Me too," said Jason.

"What have you got planned, Angel?" Daniel asked.

"Let me guess," Jason interrupted. "Playing computer games—right, Angel?"

Angel looked up from his work and grinned. "Good guess," he answered. "I'm not into winter sports. While you three are out there on the slopes, I'll be nice and cozy—playing Snowboard Safari on my laptop!"

Ten days later, it was time for the first snowboarding lesson. Daniel and Sophia pulled on their goggles, hats, and gloves, and then grabbed their boards and clumped outside. A small group was gathered nearby, and a man with a clipboard called out names.

"Daniel and Sophia Lutz?"

"Here!" Daniel and Sophia said.

"Jason Walker?"

"Here!" Jason called back.

"Angel Hernandez?"

Daniel and Sophia looked at each other in surprise.

"Angel Hernandez?" the instructor called again.

"I'm here," he said, standing next to the twins.

"I thought you didn't like winter sports," Daniel whispered.

"I don't," Angel whispered back, grumpily. "My parents didn't want me to spend the vacation in front of the computer so they gave me boarding lessons as a surprise."

The class spent the next thirty minutes in one spot. They learned how to stand, balance, and lean on the snowboard.

"Ready to try the real thing?" the instructor asked.

"Yes!" shouted most of the group.

"Not really," muttered Angel.

They followed the instructor to the drag lift that would carry each of them to the top of the beginners' slope.

"Sophia, you first," the instructor said. "Just grab the cable, lean back a little, and let it pull you up the hill."

At the top, Daniel and Sophia stood with Angel and Jason.

"Ready?" Daniel said.

"It looks steep," Angel replied.

Sophia pointed her board sideways and bent her knees. Daniel and Jason did the same. Angel just watched.

"Let's go!" Sophia said.

She slid a few yards and then fell backward into the snow.

Jason raced past her. "I'm going too fast!" he yelled. He swerved and tumbled into a snow bank.

"Not any more!" Sophia called.

Daniel laughed and then turned to Angel. "Our turn next!" he said.

But Angel shook his head. "In a minute," he replied.

Daniel pushed off to catch up with Sophia. Together, they slipped, stumbled, and rolled down the hill.

"Let's go again!" Sophia said at the bottom. When they got to the top, Angel was still waiting.

"Come on, Angel," Sophia said. "We're all hopeless!"

Angel gave a wobbly smile. He took a step forward. "I guess if you can fall down the hill, I can too." He pointed his board, bent his knees, and started to slide forward.

"That's it, Angel!" Daniel called.

"Hey, Angel!" Sophia called. "You've gone further than I did!"

But just then, Angel slipped off his board into the snow.

"Oops! He's down," said Daniel. "Let's go."

Daniel and Sophia headed down to help Angel up, but they were too slow. By the time they reached the spot where he had fallen, he was on his board again and halfway down the hill.

Sophia slid the last few yards on her knees. Daniel skidded into her and they fell in a laughing heap.

Angel walked over to them. "This is far better than Snowboard Safari," he said. "What are you waiting for? Let's go again!"

Jake's Visit

Ethan was excited. His pen pal Jake was coming to visit, all the way from Planet Yopp. Ethan and Jake kept in touch by satellite text, but today they were going to meet for the very first time.

When Jake arrived, Ethan couldn't believe his eyes. It wasn't Jake's bright green, scaly skin that surprised him, but his two heads and seven wavy tentacles.

"Bopp, gloppy dopp!" said Jake cheerfully.

Ethan looked at his dad. "What did he say?" he asked.

"You've forgotten to turn on your translator, silly," said Dad. He switched the control on Ethan's suit to "on."

"Hello, Ethan," said Jake.

Ethan could understand him now. "Hello, Jake," he replied.

It was hard finding things to do with Jake. Ethan took him roller-skating, but there weren't enough roller skates in Jake's size. They tried moon dancing, but Jake tripped everyone up.

In the end, they decided to go for a meal at Ethan's favorite restaurant, the Moon Rock Café.

Jake ate more food than Ethan would eat in a week. He gobbled up ten cosmic burgers, eight plates of meteor fries, and

six galactic fruit salads.

"Yummy!" said Jake.

Ethan wasn't so happy. He didn't have enough money left to pay for the enormous meal.

When he found out, the restaurant manager wasn't pleased. "You can do the dishes!" he said.

In the kitchen, Jake washed the dirty plates, spinning and juggling them with his tentacles. Ethan could hardly believe his eyes! In just a few minutes they had finished.

The manager was amazed. "You can both have vacation jobs if you want!" he said.

Ethan and Jake were thrilled. They were going to get paid and have a great vacation, too.

Crazy Animals

Stomp! Stomp! Zebra's proud,
Because he stands out in a crowd.

Squeak! Squeak! Little Mouse
Scampers quickly through the house.

Roar! Roar! Hear Lion roar!
Eats his lunch and still wants more!

Meow! Meow! Have you seen
Naughty Kitty licking cream?

Bark! Bark! Messy Pup!
Hides his bone, then digs it up.

Baa! Baa! Clever Sheep!
Counting lambs to fall asleep.

Elephant's Trunk

Elephant loves to blow his trunk
At the start of every day.
"Tarrantarra!" he loudly trumps,
To wake his friends to play.

Elephant's trunk is useful
To shower and to squirt.
Down at the pool his friends join in,
To wash off all the dirt.

And when it comes to mealtimes,
A trunk can help once more—
To reach the highest, juiciest leaves
That jungle friends adore.

But best of all for Elephant,
When his friends are tucked up snug,
He loves to wrap his trunk around,
And give them a big hug!

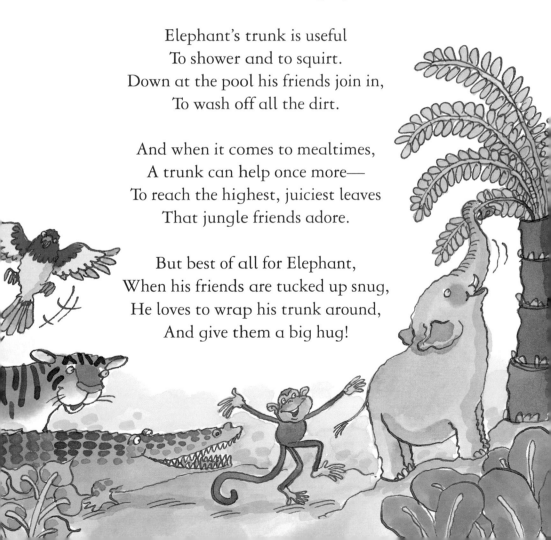

Fat Cat

David and Josh had a job feeding Fluffy, Mr. and Mrs. Cole's cat, while they went on vacation for a week.

"Don't forget, Fluffy needs to be fed three times a day," Mrs. Cole told the boys, as she handed over the huge cat.

As Mr. Cole got into the car he whispered to David and Josh, "Try not to let Fluffy eat too much!"

"Mr. Cole is right," said Josh a week later, as he and David watched Fluffy eating. "Fluffy definitely eats too much."

"Let's see if I can stop her," said David. He made a barking noise, like a dog.

David and Josh had never seen a cat move so fast. She bolted through the cat door into the back garden and up the nearest tree.

Josh and David ran outside.

"Now look what you've done, David!" said Josh.

"Don't panic, I'll get her down," said David. He went home to fetch his toy bow and arrow and a rope. Then he tied the rope to one of the arrows and fired it over a branch.

"Hold one end of the rope, Josh,"

David said. Slowly, David pulled himself up the tree using the rope. "Phew! This is hard work!" he panted.

But just as David reached the branch that Fluffy sat on, the cat scampered back down the tree trunk all by herself.

David looked down. "Oh no!" he cried. "I'm stuck now!"

"It looks like we arrived home just in time!" said Mr. Cole, walking into the garden. He put a stepladder against the tree and helped David down. "What were you doing up there?" he asked.

David and Josh explained, and Mr. Cole laughed.

When Mrs. Cole came outside she didn't find it quite so funny. "Fluffy doesn't usually climb trees," she said, cuddling the enormous cat and frowning at David and Josh.

Fluffy purred and looked smug.

"Well she should probably climb them more often," said Mr. Cole.

He turned to Josh and David. "I'm going to double your pay, for giving Fluffy some exercise!" he said. "Perhaps I'll start barking at her, too!" he joked.

Teddy Bear

Teddy Bear, Teddy Bear,
Turn around.

Teddy Bear, Teddy Bear,
Touch the ground.

Teddy Bear, Teddy Bear,
Show your shoe.

Teddy Bear, Teddy Bear,
That will do!

Teddy Bear, Teddy Bear,
Go upstairs.

Teddy Bear, Teddy Bear,
Say your prayers.

Teddy Bear, Teddy Bear,
Turn out the lights.

Teddy Bear, Teddy Bear,
Say good-night!

This Is the Way the Ladies Ride

This is the way the ladies ride:
Tri, tre, tre, tree,
Tri, tre, tre, tree!
This is the way the ladies ride:
Tri, tre, tre, tree, tri-tre-tre-tree!

This is the way the gentlemen ride:
Gallop-a-trot, Gallop-a-trot!
This is the way the gentlemen ride:
Gallop-a-gallop-a-trot!

This is the way the farmers ride:
Hobbledy-hoy,
Hobbledy-hoy!
This is the way the farmers ride:
Hobbledy hobbledy-hoy!

Rain

Rain, rain, go to Spain,
Never show your face again.

Jack-a-Dandy

Nauty pauty Jack-a-Dandy
Stole a piece of sugar candy
From the local candy store,
And ran away out of the door.

Tomorrow Is a Special Day

Tomorrow is a special day,
I'm off on vacation—hooray!
I'm going where there's sand and sea,
And lots of treats for you and me,
Where ponies give rides on the beach,
And seagulls fly just out of reach.

My Aunt

I'm glad I've got an aunt,
She really is a winner.
She takes me out to feed the ducks,
And then she makes me dinner.

Marching

March, march, head erect,
Left, right, that's correct.

King Boggen

King Boggen, he built a fine new hall;
Pastry and piecrust, that was the wall;
The windows were made of black pudding and white,
Roofed with pancakes—you never saw the like.

The Gadget Meeting

"Can I have a new cell phone for my birthday?" Jed asked Mom. "One that takes photos and plays music? Some even have a TV screen!" he added hopefully. Jed loved gadgets.

Mom looked up from her computer. "Have you seen how much they cost?" she said. "I'm sorry, Jed, they're just too expensive."

Jed sighed loudly. It was OK for Mom, he thought. She was a spy for top-secret government agency Unit X, so she could use cool gadgets whenever she liked. It was part of her job.

"Time for dinner," said Mom. She stood up and went quickly downstairs to the kitchen.

Jed sat down at the computer, wondering if the screen would show him Mom's latest mission.

It didn't. The e-mail on screen was from Aunt Kathy, asking Mom what to get Jed for his birthday. Jed thought about the idea of replying as Mom and suggesting a new cell phone.

He grinned. Better not.

Just then, Jed noticed an e-mail marked *Top Secret* higher up in Mom's in-box. He clicked on it.

Dear Agent
The latest spy tools and gadgets will be shown tomorrow.
Time: 2:00 p.m., Saturday July 16th
Place: The Martin Luther King Room, Bristol Hotel,
14th Street Southeast, Washington
All agents must attend.

"Wow…" Jed sighed. "Lucky Mom!" he thought.

"Hurry up, Jed!" shouted Mom.

Jed jumped—and accidentally clicked on "Delete."

"Oh no!" he gasped. He hoped that Mom would remember the address in the e-mail. Jed couldn't tell her, or she would guess what he had been up to!

The next morning Mom looked very worried.

"Are you going to work today, Mom?" Jed asked.

Mom shook her head. Jed felt very guilty indeed.

Then he had an idea. If he couldn't tell her where the secret meeting was, maybe he could show her.

"Can we go on a bus tour around Washington?" he asked.

"It's a lovely sunny day."

"OK, Jed," said Mom. "It might cheer me up."

The bus tour went on a loop, passing all the famous landmarks. As the bus got close to the Capitol, Jed wondered if his plan would work. He looked at his watch. It was ten to two. Just then, Mom gasped. She was staring at the Bristol Hotel. She had remembered!

"Jed, I've just seen some friends from work I want to say hello to," she said, standing up. "Stay on the bus and see the rest of the tour. I'll meet you back here."

"OK, Mom," said Jed, smiling as she hurried off the bus. "See you later."

But Jed got off the bus at the next stop. He walked back up 14th Street and into the Bristol Hotel. "I'll just have to make sure Mom doesn't see me in here!" he said.

Jed had the best time trying out some amazing gadgets. "This is even better than that cell phone I wanted," he said, picking up a satellite tracking device. He typed in Mom's name—and a picture of her came up on the screen. She was standing at the bus stop outside!

"Oops, I'd better go!" he said. He put the gadget down and hurried out. "Hi, Mom!" he said, tapping her on the back.

"Where have you been?" she cried. "The bus came, but you weren't on it!"

"Sorry, Mom," Jed replied. "I suddenly got motion sickness so I got off a couple of stops early. I had to walk all the way up 14th Street!"

Jed's mom gave him a hug. "You poor thing!" she said. "I know, let's go to the movies. There's a new spy movie showing that I've heard is really good."

"Great!" Jed agreed. This had turned out to be the best day ever!

Old Roger Is Dead

Old Roger is dead and gone to his grave,
H'm ha! gone to his grave.

They planted an apple tree over his head,
H'm ha! over his head.

The apples were ripe and ready to fall,
H'm ha! ready to fall.

There came an old woman and picked them all up,
H'm ha! picked them all up.

Old Roger jumped up and gave her a knock,
H'm ha! gave her a knock.

Which made the old woman go hippity hop,
H'm ha! hippity hop!

My Funny Family

My aunt May's got a brain like a sieve—
She forgets where the things in her kitchen all live.
There are plates in the refridgerator and jam in the jug
A chop in the teapot and carrots in the mugs!

My cousin Jack's got eyes like a hawk—
He can see across the ocean from London to New York!
He says he can see unknown planets orbiting in space
And the moon has a handlebar moustache upon its face.

My sister Sarah's got feet that love to dance—
She's danced from Perth to Benidorm, from Italy to France.
She dances in a dress trimmed with black-and-yellow lace,
Mom says she looks just like a bee and that it's a disgrace!

My dog Joshua's got a ferocious appetite—
To see him eating up his food is really quite a sight.
He wolfs down chips and when he's really feeling gross,
He'll polish off a cake and several rounds of buttered toast!

Pet Prize

It was school fair day. There was going to be a Best Pet Competition.

Tom's friends all brought their pets. Sammy had a hamster. Carlos had an orange cat. Deepak had his rabbit, Sooty.

"I wish I had a pet," said Tom. Miss Bell was going to judge the competition. Her dog Chip had come, too.

Chip was small and brown and had a very waggy tail.

"Can I pet him?" asked Tom.

"Yes," said Miss Bell. "He's very friendly."

Tom petted Chip. Chip wagged his tail furiously.

"I wish I had a pet like you," whispered Tom to Chip.

Chip barked understandingly.

Miss Bell looked at the pets.

She looked at a rabbit, two hamsters, four gerbils, one cat, three mice, two dogs…

"And the prize for best-groomed pet goes to… Carlos!" she said, giving him a medal.

Sammy won the prize for friendliest pet.

Deepak won the prize for most well-behaved pet.

Tom wished more and more that he had a pet of his own to enter in the competition.

Then Miss Bell looked around. "Where is Chip?" she asked. Chip was missing!

"We must find him!" said Miss Bell. She was very worried.

"I'll go and look for him," said Tom.

He looked at the book stall. Chip wasn't there.

He looked at the raffle stall. Chip wasn't there either.

Then Tom saw a wagging tail. He looked under the cake stall—and there was Chip, licking up the crumbs!

Chip wagged his tail when he saw Tom and barked.

"Time to go back," said Tom.

At the end of the competition, Miss Bell gave out a special prize.

"And this prize is for Best Pet Finder," she said with a smile. "The winner is... Tom!"

A Boy's Song

Where the pools are bright and deep,
Where the gray trout lies asleep,
Up the river and over the lea,
That's the way for Billy and me.

Where the blackbird sings the latest,
Where the hawthorn blooms the sweetest,
Where the nestlings chirp and flee,
That's the way for Billy and me.

Where the mowers mow the cleanest,
Where the hay lies thick and greenest,
There to track the homeward bee,
That's the way for Billy and me.

Where the hazel bank is steepest,
Where the shadow falls the deepest,
Where the clustering nuts fall free,
That's the way for Billy and me.

Why the boys should drive away
Little sweet maidens from the play,
Or love to banter and fight so well,
That's the thing I never could tell.

But this I know, I love to play
Through the meadow, among the hay;
Up the water and over the lea,
That's the way for Billy and me.

I'll Show You How

Oakey and Dad were walking through the woods.

"Hello!" said Squirrel. "Would you like to play?"

"All right," smiled Oakey.

"Let's climb some trees," suggested Squirrel, but Oakey wasn't sure.

"What if I fall?" he asked.

"Don't worry," Squirrel told him. "I'll show you how to do it."

And he showed Oakey what to do.

Dad nodded to Oakey. "You can try. Go ahead."

So Oakey gave it a try. "This really is fun!" he laughed.

"What's all the noise?" said a voice. Dormouse poked her head through the leaves.

"Have you come to play?"

"Um… all right," mumbled Oakey.

"Good! Let's swing from this branch," suggested Dormouse.

But Oakey wasn't sure. "What if I get it wrong?" he asked.

"Don't worry about getting it wrong," Dormouse smiled. "I'll show you how to do it." And she did.

"I'm enjoying it!" Oakey laughed.

"Well then, come and play with me," said a voice. "And you'll really have a good time."

Oakey looked down. Otter was watching from under the tree. "Follow me!" he called.

So Oakey and his friends ran after Otter to the river.

"Let's swim," said Otter.

But Oakey wasn't sure. "I've never tried it before," he said.

"I'll show you how to do it," said Otter.

Dad nodded to Oakey. "You can try. Go ahead."

"You'll have a great time, I promise!" Otter said.

And Oakey did!

"Now it's time for my game," Oakey told his friends. "Let's play leapfrog."

"Oh dear!" said Squirrel. "I've never tried this."

"Neither have I," added Dormouse. "I'm not sure."

"Me neither," agreed Otter.

"What if we're not very good?" they all said at once.

"You should always try," Oakey encouraged them. "You showed me that trying something new is fun. And besides, good friends will show you how it's done!"

Don't Be Scared

"Little Cub," said Dad, "I think the time's right for you to come out with me to explore tonight."

Little Cub peered at the evening sky. The sun was slipping down behind the trees. Shadows stretched across the plain.

As they set off, Little Cub shivered, and suddenly stopped.

"What's that high up there in that tree?" he asked. "There are two great big eyes watching me."

"Look closer, Little Cub. That thing up there is just old Owl. Did he give you a scare?" asked Dad.

"Dad," smiled Little Cub, "Owl won't give me a scare. He can't do that, as long as you're there."

Suddenly, Little Cub stopped. "What's that black shape hanging down from that tree? I felt it reaching out for me."

"Look closer, Little Cub. That thing up there is just old Snake. Did he give you a scare?" asked Dad.

"Dad," smiled Little Cub, "Snake won't give me a scare. He can't do that, as long as you're there."

Dad and Little Cub walked on. Suddenly, Little Cub stopped.

"What's that I can hear

behind that tree? There's
a huge black shadow
following us."

"Look closer, Little Cub. That
thing back there is just old Elephant. Did he give you a scare?"
asked Dad.

"Dad," smiled Little Cub, "Elephant won't give me a scare.
He can't do that, as long as you're there."

Dad and Little Cub walked on. Suddenly, Dad stopped.

"What's that?" he asked.

"Toowhit, toowhoo! Sssss, Sssss! Terummmp, terummmp!"

The animals jumped out at Dad. Dad jumped!

"Don't be scared," laughed Little Cub.

"Sorry, Lion! Did we give you a fright?" asked the animals,
laughing.

"No!" said Dad. "You couldn't give me a scare. Not as long
as Little Cub is there."

Then, side by side, Little Cub and Dad headed for home.

Midnight Fun

Just as midnight's striking,
When everyone's asleep,
Teddies yawn and stretch and shake,
And out of warm beds creep.

They sneak out from their houses,
And gather in the dark,
Then skip along the empty streets,
Heading for the park.

And there beneath the moonlight,
They tumble down the slides,
They swoosh up high upon the swings,
And play on all the rides.

And when the sun comes peeping,
They rush home to their beds,
And snuggle down as children wake,
To cuddle with their teds!

Farm Hide-and-Seek

Standing in the meadow,
Underneath the tree,
Chewing, mooing, munching,
Who can it be?

Over in the barnyard,
By the mommy sheep,
Small and white and woolly,
Who's fast asleep?

Right inside the henhouse,
Glowing in the sun,
Fluffy, bright, and yellow,
Who's about to run?

Over in the paddock,
Running wild and free,
Galloping and trotting,
Who can you see?

Past the grassy meadow,
In the field beyond,
Flapping wings and quacking,
Who's in the pond?

Green Cheese

Green cheese,
Yellow laces,
Up and down
The market places.

Pit, Pat

Pit, pat, well-a-day,
Little Robin flew away;
Where can little robin be?
Gone into the cherry tree.

The Wind

Who has seen the wind? Neither I nor you;
But when the leaves hang trembling
The wind is passing through.

Who has seen the wind? Neither you nor I;
But when the trees bow down their heads
The wind is passing by.

Bagpipes

Puss came dancing out of a barn
With a pair of bagpipes under her arm;
She could sing nothing but, "Fiddle cum fee,
The mouse has married the humble bee."
Pipe, cat! Dance, mouse!
We'll have a wedding at our good house.

Mother?

"Mother, may I go out to swim?"
"Yes, my darling daughter.
Fold your clothes up neat and trim,
But don't go near the water."

Shrovetide

Once, twice, thrice,
I give thee warning,
Please to make pancakes
Again in the morning.

Here Is the Church

Here is the church, *(link hands)*

Here is the steeple, *(put index fingers together)*

Look inside, *(keeping your hands linked, turn them upside down)*

Here are the people! *(wiggle your fingers)*

Once I Was a Baby

Once I was a baby,
Now suddenly, I'm big!
And there's someone else
Sleeping in my crib.
Mom says it's my new brother,
He's very small and sweet,
With hands the size of daisies
And very smooth, pink feet.
I think I'm going to like him,
And I know that he'll like me.
Won't it be terrific
When I can hold him on my knee?

The Work of Art

David had a bright idea. "Let's put a notice on the school noticeboard," he said. *"David and Josh's Odd Job Service—No job too big or too small."*

"Let's do it!" said Josh.

On Thursday afternoon, Miss Price, the principal of the nursery next door, called the boys into her office. "I've seen your notice," she told them. "I have a job for you. I'd like you to paint the nursery playground wall."

"When can we start?" asked Josh.

"Tomorrow after school," said Miss Price.

After school the next day, the janitor carried some paint cans and paintbrushes into the playground.

"Miss Price didn't say what color she wanted the wall to be painted," the janitor said, opening the cans of paint. "I'll leave you to choose." Then he went back into his shed at the side of the playground.

David and Josh looked at the paints. There was red, yellow, green, and purple paint.

"We should use all the colors to paint a huge picture," said David.

Josh nodded. "Let's paint some baseball players," he suggested, picking up a pot of green paint.

"No, some monsters," said David, taking a can of purple paint.

"Baseball players!" said Josh.

"Monsters!" argued David. He flicked some purple paint at the wall.

"Baseball players! " yelled Josh, flicking some green paint over David's purple paint.

By the time Josh and David had finished arguing, the whole wall was splattered with purple and green, and there wasn't a monster or a baseball player in sight.

"Oh dear!" said Josh, staring at the wall.

They left the paints and hurried off home.

First thing on Monday morning, Josh and David were called in to see Miss Price.

Miss Price was quiet for a moment. Then she clapped her hands in delight. "Well done!" she said. "What a fantastic piece of modern art!"

David and Josh grinned at each other as Miss Price handed them an envelope.

"Here's your money for a job well done!" she said.

Hansel and Gretel

Hansel and Gretel lived by the forest with their father, a poor woodcutter, and their stepmother.

One evening, the family had nothing left to eat but a few crusts of bread. Hansel and Gretel went to bed hungry. As they lay in their beds, they heard the grownups talking.

"There are too many mouths to feed," said their stepmother. "We must take your children into the forest and leave them there."

"Never!" cried their father.

But the next morning, Hansel and Gretel's stepmother woke them early.

"Get up!" she ordered. "We're going into the forest to chop wood."

She handed them each a crust of bread for their lunch.

Hansel broke his bread into tiny pieces in his pocket, and as they walked, he secretly dropped a trail of crumbs on the ground.

Deep in the forest, Hansel and Gretel's father built them a fire.

"We are going to chop wood now," he said. "We'll return at sunset."

After awhile, the children shared Gretel's bread, and then they curled up at the foot of an old oak tree and fell asleep.

When Hansel and Gretel woke up, they looked for the trail of breadcrumbs, but they were gone! The forest birds had eaten them.

"We'll wait till morning," Hansel said. "Then we can find our way home."

The next morning, the children walked through the forest, until they came to a little house made of gingerbread! The roof was dripping with sugary icing, the door was made of candy canes, and the garden was filled with colorful lollipops.

Delighted, the hungry children began to feast upon the sweets. As they ate, an old woman hobbled out of the house.

"You must be starving, my dears," she said. "Come inside and have a proper meal."

The old woman fed them well and then put them to bed.

But Hansel and Gretel didn't know that the kind old woman was really a wicked witch. As she watched them sleep, she cackled, "I'll soon fatten these two up. Then they will make a proper meal for me!"

The following morning, the witch dragged Hansel from his bed, and threw him into a cage. Then she made Gretel cook her brother a big breakfast.

"Your brother is too skinny," the witch told Gretel. "I'll keep him locked up until he is nice and plump, and then I'll eat him up!"

Over the next few days, Hansel had as much food as he could eat. And every morning, the witch made him stick out his finger so she could feel whether he was fat enough to eat.

But Hansel knew that the old witch could hardly see, so he stuck a chicken bone through the cage instead.

"Still too scrawny," the witch would say.

One day, the witch got tired of waiting and decided to eat Hansel right away.

"Light the oven!" the witch ordered Gretel. "Now crawl in and see if it's hot enough."

Gretel knew the witch was planning to cook her as well. So she decided to trick the witch.

"The oven's much too small for me," she said.

"Nincompoop!" cried the witch. "Even I could get into that oven. Look!" And she stuck her head inside.

With a great big shove, Gretel pushed the witch into the oven and slammed the door shut.

Gretel freed Hansel from his cage, and they danced happily around the kitchen. "We're safe! We're safe!" they sang. When the children looked around the witch's house, they found chests crammed with gold and sparkling jewels. They filled their pockets and set off for home.

They seemed to find their way straight home, where their delighted father greeted them with hugs and kisses.

He told them that their cruel stepmother had died, so they had nothing to fear. Hansel and Gretel showed him the treasure they had found.

"We will never go hungry again!" they said. They all lived happily ever after.

Best Friends

Brandon and Paul were best friends. They sat next to each other in class every day. They played together and ate lunch together every day.

One day at break, Brandon pulled Paul's coat and a button flew off.

Paul and Brandon looked for the button all through recess, but they couldn't find it anywhere.

Then the bell rang to say that recess time was over.

"We *must* find my button," said Paul, "or my mom will be really mad!" So Brandon and Paul kept looking until they found the button.

Miss Bell told them off for being late.

"It's your fault!" Paul said to Brandon.

"It's your fault!" Brandon said to Paul.

The two friends did not talk to each other in class for the rest of the morning. They did not sit together at lunch.

The first lesson after lunch was gym.

"Let's see who can change the most quickly!" Miss Bell said.

Brandon and Paul pulled out their gym bags.

"I'm going to beat Paul," Brandon thought to himself. "I'll show him!"

"I'm going to beat Brandon," Paul thought to himself. "That'll serve him right!"

The two boys raced to change into their shorts and T-shirts.

They finished at exactly the same time.

"I'm first!" cried Brandon, raising his hand. His T-shirt suddenly felt very tight under the arms.

"No, I'm first!" shouted Paul. As he raised his hand as well, he suddenly noticed that his T-shirt was almost down to his knees.

"Why are your clothes so small, Brandon?" asked Billy.

"And why are yours so big, Paul?" asked Miss Bell.

Their friends started to laugh. "You mixed up your gym bags!" said Tilly, pointing at the two bags.

Brandon and Paul laughed as well.

"Friends again?" said Brandon.

"Friends again!" said Paul.

Did You See My Wife?

Did you see my wife, did you see, did you see,
Did you see my wife looking for me?
She wears a straw bonnet, with white ribbands on it,
And diminity petticoats over her knee.

Punctuate

Every lady in this land
Has twenty nails upon each hand.
Five and twenty on hands and feet
All this is true without deceit.

Simple Simon

Simple Simon met a pie man
Going to the fair;
Said Simple Simon to the pie man,
"Let me taste your ware."

Said the pieman to Simple Simon,
"Show me first your penny;"
Said Simple Simon to the pie man,
"Indeed I have not any."

Peter, Peter, Pumpkin Eater

Peter, Peter, pumpkin eater,
Had a wife and couldn't keep her;
He put her in a pumpkin shell
And there he kept her very well.

Billy Booster

Billy Billy Booster,
Had a little rooster,
The rooster died
And Billy cried.
Poor Billy Booster.

Tommy Snooks and Bessy Brooks

As Tommy Snooks and Bessy Brooks
Were walking out one Sunday,
Says Tommy Snooks to Bessy Brooks,
"Tomorrow will be Monday."

Raindrops

I love to see the raindrops
Splashing on the sidewalks;
I love to see the sunlight
Twinkling in the rain;
I love to see the wind gusts
Drying up the raindrops;
I love to feel the sunshine
Coming out again!

The Dark Wood

In the dark, dark wood, there was a dark, dark house.
And in that dark, dark house there was a dark, dark room,
And in that dark, dark room, there was a dark, dark closet,
And in that dark, dark closet there was a dark, dark shelf,
And on that dark, dark shelf there was a dark, dark box,
And in that dark, dark box, there was a GHOST!

Gym Giraffe

Jeremy Giraffe loved going out with his dad to gather juicy green leaves for dinner.

"Remember—the tallest trees have the tastiest leaves, and the tiny top leaves are the tenderest!" his dad would say.

One morning Jeremy decided he wanted to gather leaves on his own, but his neck wouldn't stretch high enough. So Jeremy went back home with his neck hanging down in despair.

"Why, Jeremy, whatever is the matter?" asked his mom. When Jeremy told her, she gave his neck a nuzzle.

"You're still growing," she assured him. But Jeremy couldn't wait for his neck to grow. So he headed to the Jungle Gym to do neck lengthening exercises.

Jeremy spent the next few weeks stretching his neck with all sorts of exercises. Finally, he felt ready to reach for the highest leaves.

Next time Jeremy and his dad went out leaf gathering, Jeremy saw some juicy leaves at the top of a very tall tree.

"I'm getting those," he said.

"They're so high up!" said Dad. But sure enough, after a big, big stretch, Jeremy reached up and ate them up!

Monkey Mayhem

Mickey, Mandy, and Maxine Monkey had finished their breakfast of Mango Munch. Now they were rushing off to play.

"Be careful!" called their mom. "And *don't* make too much noise!"

"We won't!" the three mischievous monkeys promised, leaping across to the next tree. The noise echoed through the whole jungle—Mickey, Mandy, and Maxine just didn't know how to be quiet!

Mickey landed on a branch. Maxine and Mandy landed beside him. Just then the branch snapped in two and they shrieked, as they went tumbling down, down, down.

The jungle shook as the three monkeys crashed to the ground, then sprang to their feet.

"Yippee!" the monkeys cheered, brushing themselves off.

The three monkeys then scrambled back up to the top of the trees. They screeched and screamed as they swung through the branches back toward home.

All through the jungle, the animals covered their ears. Nobody would ever keep these three noisy monkeys quiet!

The Double Agent

Jed was playing in an important soccer game at school.

"I'll come and watch!" Mom said that morning, as she left for work. But when Jed scanned the crowd of cheering parents, his mom was nowhere to be seen. Elise was there instead.

"Where's Mom?" Jed asked, when the game was over. His team had lost 3-0, and Jed was in a bad mood.

"She called to say she had to stay at work," Elise replied.

That evening, Mom didn't get home until after Jed's bedtime. She came in and sat down on Jed's bed. "I'm really sorry about not coming to your soccer game, Jed," she said. "There are problems at work. I might lose my job if things don't get better." She looked tired and worried.

Jed stopped feeling angry. Mom needs my help, he thought.

Later that night, Jed crept downstairs into the study. He clicked on Mom's in-box to see what had been happening.

The latest e-mail in there was from Chief Officer Gridlock, Mom's boss at Unit X, the government's top spy agency.

Dear Agent
I am sorry to inform you that more government secrets have been leaked to the newspapers. You have failed in your mission to root out the double agent at Unit X. I am taking you off the case.
Gridlock

Jed sighed. Things really were bad for Mom.

The next morning, Jed didn't turn up for his paper round. Instead, he rode his bicycle to Unit X. I'm going to have a good snoop around, he thought.

Jed slipped past the security guard and up the stairs. He soon found Chief Officer Gridlock's office, but Jed could tell that Chief Officer Gridlock was already inside. There was a light shining under his door.

Jed waited around the corner. After a few minutes, Gridlock's door opened. A fierce-looking man came out and walked across the corridor to the bathroom.

Jed followed. Now's my chance, he thought, as Gridlock shut the door. Jed wedged a chair under the door handle.

"Who's that?"
shouted Gridlock.
"Let me out!"

Jed ran back to
Gridlock's office.
There wasn't a
moment to lose.

The computer was

the best place to start looking. He needed a list of all the
people who worked at Unit X. Gridlock had been checking his
e-mails, and had left them up on his screen. Jed clicked on the
"Sent" button.

He took a deep breath. "Gridlock doesn't know much about
computers!" he said. "He sends his e-mails to every one of his
contact—even the national newspaper editors. So he's the
one who is accidentally giving away all the secrets!"

Suddenly a hand gripped Jed's shoulder.
Gridlock wasn't the boss of Unit X
for nothing—he had escaped from
the toilet.

"Who on earth are you? I'm calling
security!" Gridlock growled.

"Go on then. I'll show them what
you've done!" said Jed. "I know
that you are the only double agent
around here. These e-mails prove it!"

Jed showed Gridlock what he'd found.

Gridlock sat down heavily in his chair. "I didn't mean to!" he groaned. "I've never understood computers."

"Then perhaps you should retire, and let someone take over who does," replied Jed. "And I know someone perfect for the job: Agent Frances Best."

Jed walked to the door. "If you don't tell on me, then I won't tell on you," he said. And then he hurried out.

That evening, Mom came home from work in a very happy mood. "I've gotten a big promotion, Jed!" she told him.

Jed gave her a hug. "Well done, Mom!" he said. Now he could look forward to some even more exciting missions.

"I couldn't have done it without you, Jed," Mom went on.

You don't know how true that is! Jed thought with a grin.

Little Tommy Tucker

Little Tommy Tucker sings for his supper.
What shall we give him?
Brown bread and butter.
How shall he cut it without a knife?
How can he marry without a wife?

A Girl Named Mag

There was a girl named Mag with feet so large
That people cried, "They're as big as a barge!"
She wished for little feet, small and round,
But when she got them, she kept falling down.

Good Night

Good night, God bless you,
Go to bed and undress you.
Good night, sweet repose,
Half the bed and all the clothes.

When Jacky's a Good Boy

When Jacky's a very good boy,
He shall have cakes and a custard;
But when he does nothing but cry,
He shall have nothing but mustard.

The Priest

The little priest of Felton,
The little priest of Felton,
He killed a mouse within his house,
And nobody there to help him.

My Shadow

I have a little shadow that goes in and out with me,
And what can be the use of him is more than I can see.
He is very, very like me from the heels up to the head;
And I see him jump before me, when I jump into my bed.

One morning, very early, before the sun was up,
I rose and found the shining dew on every buttercup;
But my lazy little shadow, like an errant sleepyhead,
Had stayed at home behind me and was fast asleep in bed.

The Egyptian Job

David and Josh were counting all the money they had made by doing odd jobs.

"It's nowhere near enough to buy our bikes yet," David said gloomily.

His mom came into the room. "I've got another odd job for you both!" she said. "I need people to hand out fliers tomorrow." David's mom ran the store at the local museum.

The next morning, David and Josh went to the museum with David's mom.

She gave them a big pile of fliers about the new Egyptian mummy exhibition.

"Give these to the people walking past," she said.

It was a freezing cold day. David and Josh were soon cold and fed up.

"My fingers are like blocks of ice!" moaned Josh.

"Let's go inside," said David. "We can hide in the bathroom while we get warm again."

A cleaning trolley had been left in the bathroom. On top of it were two huge rolls of toilet paper.

David looked at Josh and grinned. He picked up one of the rolls and began to wrap it around and around Josh.

"This will keep you

warm!" he joked.

When David had finished, Josh could hardly move.

"You look very funny!" laughed David, as he gave Josh a friendly push.

Josh lost his balance and fell against the bathroom door. The door opened and he staggered through it. "Help!" he yelled.

In front of him, a mummy display case was open. Two robbers were about to steal the priceless mummy.

"Aaargh!" screamed the robbers, seeing Josh. "That mummy has come to life!"

Josh, who was still trying to regain his balance, staggered toward them.

"Quick! Let's get out of here!" the robbers cried.

The manager hurried over to Josh and David. "You've saved our prize exhibit!" he said. "You deserve a reward! I shall write you each a check for $200."

"Fantastic!" said Josh.

"Now we have enough money to buy those bikes we want!" said David.

Little Ghost Lost

"Come along, Eric," said Mom. "It's time we took you out for your first proper spooking expedition. And what better night for spooking than Halloween!"

"Just follow us and copy what we do," said Dad. "And don't wander off on your own."

The three ghosts floated up the chimney of their home in the Haunted House, and curled out of the top like wisps of smoke.

"I don't like it out here," said Eric, timidly. "It's too dark!"

"Don't be silly," said Mom. "Ghosts aren't afraid of the dark!"

All through the evening the family of ghosts played ghostly pranks, jumping out and spooking folk, and squealing with delight as they ran away, screaming.

"I bet I could spook someone all on my own!" thought Eric.

Creeping up behind two children, he set his face in its most fearsome expression, then tapped them on their shoulders. But, as the children spun around, Eric froze in horror. He was eye to eye with two gruesome monsters!

Eric screeched and fled into the night. He didn't hear the screams behind him, or see the monsters race home, where they tore off their Halloween masks and panted out their story to their mother. Poor Eric had never heard of trick-or-treating!

Eric flitted down the streets, calling for

his mom and dad. Where had he left them? Finally
he sank down in a doorway.

"I want my mom!" he wailed, and
began to cry. Then something poked and
prodded him with a sharp stick.

"What have we here then?" said a
mean little voice.

"Looks like a young ghostie. Let's
pinch him!" said another nasty voice.
The voices belonged to two goblins.

"*Boo!*" said Eric, pulling a scary face.
"Leave me alone!"

But the goblins just burst out laughing. It takes
a lot to frighten a goblin. "Nothing scares us!" they teased.

"Oh no?" said a deep voice behind them. "How about this!"
The goblins turned to see two huge, terrifying ghosts.
"Aaaaargh!" they cried, fleeing into the night.
"Mom! Dad!" cried Eric in delight. "You found me!"

Safely back in the Haunted House,
Eric said, miserably, "I'm never going
to make a good spook!"

"Yes you will," soothed Mom, tucking
him into bed. "After all, you certainly
scared us! Next time, stick close!"

"I promise," said Eric, and in no
time at all he was sound asleep,
dreaming of ways to spook goblins.

Index

Index